ASYLUM

ASYLUM

Nan Corbitt Allen

MOODY PUBLISHERS

CHICAGO

© 2004 by
NAN CORBITT ALLEN

All Scripture quotations are taken from the King James Version.

ISBN 0-7394-4029-2

Printed in the United States of America

*To the Lord who inspires and sustains me daily
and whose mercy to me is beyond words.*

*To my precious family:
Dennis, my husband,
who encouraged me to write this story down,
and who believes I can do anything I put my mind to;
my sons, Mark and Drew,
young men who have truly made their mother proud;
my daughter-in-law, Kelly,
who has been a breath of fresh air to our family.*

*In memory of my parents: Comer and Smitty—
I know they would be so proud.*

Acknowledgments

Many thanks to my sister, June, who helped me with law enforcement jargon and contacts; to John Dennis of the Jackson County, Florida, Sheriff's Department; and to Mary and Dunc Kelly, who gave me information on Mobile.

Prologue

Fire, fire/Flames get higher. Fire, fire/Flames get higher.
Ian closed his eyes and jumped.

Chapter One

A hot wind blew,

ruffling the leaves of the sprays on the two caskets. Ian's summer wool suit pants itched, and the new dress shoes he wore, bought that day by his great-aunt Jo, had already rubbed a blister on his left heel.

His bony frame didn't wear the suit well. He felt as if he had been placed in a large sack and was being challenged to punch his way out. The new haircut made his neck feel prickly too. With that and the wool and the shoes, he couldn't remember ever feeling so uncomfortable. But his discomfort served as a distraction, for which he was grateful. *Itchy clothes/So it goes,* he said to himself.

He had only met Aunt Jo two days before. He knew she existed, though. She had sent him a ten-dollar bill for his tenth birthday last October. Of course, if Ian hadn't retrieved the mail every day from the mailbox himself, he might have never gotten it, he figured. Maybe Aunt Jo had sent him other gifts, gifts that he'd never received, gifts that his parents had intercepted through the years. Since he had started doing everything around the house himself, he was finding a lot of things he had never known before. He had learned to cook, to clean, to do laundry, and to be very quiet when his parents were drinking, which recently had been most of the time.

Ian gazed at the two coffins in front of him. They were smooth and shiny, almost pretty. He was suddenly glad that his parents' final rest would be in a place so lovely and not littered with whiskey bottles, cigarettes, and the stench of their own bodies. He wanted to touch the coffins, like one final caress of his mother's hair, one farewell pat on his father's back. He didn't dare, though. He couldn't remember the last time he'd touched them or been touched by them tenderly. *A final touch? That's too much.*

"Ashes to ashes, dust to dust," the pastor said piously. Ian snapped back to the sound of the minister's voice. *Ashes!* He almost laughed. It was an ironic eulogy for his two dead parents. If they'd died in an auto accident or by natural causes, it would not have seemed amusing. But these two had perished in a house fire. Ian looked up at the reverend and at the faces of the small somber group: Aunt Jo; Nick and Trooper; two drinking buddies of his parents; the reverend's wife, and the reverend himself. No one else had caught the joke.

Ian's parents, Ed and Mary Lane, had never set foot in the pastor's church, and they had made no secret of their distrust of organized religion and the clergy. The pastor's occasional visits to the house were usually met with drunken ramblings or angry curses. Ian knew that this man's services and last words at their funeral were strained and obligatory.

Sweat trickled down Ian's face. Or was it a tear?

Ian hadn't talked to anyone about that night. He had

only remembered some of it. No one had helped him fill in the empty spaces. All he knew was that his parents were dead, his heel throbbed, he itched all over, and he would probably go to live with his aunt Jo in another town.

Ian tuned out the next recitation of Scripture. Instead, he remembered a poem he'd had to memorize at school, "Where Go the Boats" by Robert Louis Stevenson.

Dark brown is the river,
Golden is the sand.
It flows along for ever,
With trees on either hand.

Green leaves a-floating,
Castles of the foam,
Boats of mine a-boating—
Where will all come home?

He loved the sentiment, the idea of drifting away on a river going somewhere, anywhere. It painted pictures in his mind of endless miles of escape to grand and glorious castles. He loved the way it felt to think of it. But Ian loved the rhyme and the meter of poems too, and he often made up his own poems to certain rhythms. Sometimes it was to his walking pace or to the cadence of his endless cleaning chores in his own house. Scrubbing the bathtub, he'd say, "Scrub, scrub/Scrub the tub/This is the way/We clean today/Sponge, sponge/Get the grunge/So Mom and Dad/Won't get so mad."

"Rock of Ages, cleft for me/Let me hide myself in thee" the pastor's wife's contralto voice began with a hard vibrato. Though he'd never heard the song before, Ian liked the rhyme. He made a promise to himself to find the place to hide that the song lyric talked about.

There had been no wake, no church service, only the graveside memorial. In Madison, people always came out for funerals. In some cases, they were almost political rallies. In others, they were gossip sessions. Sometimes they were sincere expressions of grief and condolence followed by a gathering at the home of the family or the deceased. Food abounded—comfort food—and reflection on the departed's influence on the community always followed the graveside service.

However, there was no house to go back to, no family to gather, no food or remembrance for Ed and Mary. After the final "amen," Ian climbed into the late-model Chevy with his great-aunt Jo and rode silently down I-10 to her home in Crestview.

The clapboard house was neat as a pin. The shrubbery that lined the front of the house was evenly manicured. The azaleas had long since bloomed, but the foliage had been pruned to perfection. The crepe myrtles at the corners of the house were still heavy with white flowers. Ian's own yard had not been well maintained, but Ian liked the lone crepe myrtle bush there. He liked to play with the tiny berries that hid a surprise. When he'd squeeze them, a tender shirred bloom would emerge, and he could smell the sweetness of it. He loved the way that life sprang forth from a tiny unassuming pod on a tree.

Ian didn't see any playground equipment at his aunt's house. No slides or tree houses anywhere, just a large painted swing hanging by two chains from the eaves of the front porch. Apparently, Aunt Jo had not housed children in recent years, or ever. Behind the house, however, was an outbuilding, a garage or storage shed that looked interesting. It had two doors on the front with a u-shaped handle on each. Threaded through the handles was a rusty chain that was bound end to end by a padlock. Ian guessed that the shed was off-limits to him or anybody else except the keeper of the key.

"Do you live here by yourself?" Ian finally asked as he passed through the front door.

"Yes, hon. Your uncle Harlan passed away five years ago. I'm by myself now. You'd have liked your uncle Harlan. He was a good man." Aunt Jo began to ramble on about her husband of thirty-five years. Ian only partially listened. His uncle had owned a small feed-and-seed store in Crestview, it seemed, and he'd been the county horseshoe pitcher at the river festival every year. Though he wasn't sick a day in his life, she said, they found him slumped over his desk at the store, dead of an apparent heart attack. Her voice trailed off a bit. Ian looked at his great-aunt and saw her wiping her eyes with a tissue.

"We never had children of our own, but your mother was like . . ." Jo stopped and reevaluated where this conversation might go. She reached over and combed through Ian's hair with her fingers.

Finally Aunt Jo directed him to a large room with a bed with an iron headboard, a small dresser, and a chifforobe. The bed looked comfortable and clean. It had two large pillows and a white chenille bedspread.

"This is your room now, Ian," Aunt Jo said in a sweet voice. "Let's get some air moving in here." She turned on a large window fan, and a warm breeze caressed Ian's face. He wondered if the old house had air-conditioning.

"Now you can put your clothes away there in the dresser and then put your little suitcase in the chifforobe. Hang up your good suit, sweet, and it'll stay nice for Sunday school. You go ahead and change while I get us something yummy to eat. I'll meet you on the porch in a jiffy," Aunt Jo said, leaving the room.

Ian opened the suitcase. These weren't his clothes. He'd never seen them before. Then he remembered. Except for what he had had on that night, all his clothes had burned. He took one item at a time out of the suitcase, looking at it and smelling it. Apparently Aunt Jo had bought these for him at the same time she had bought the uncomfortable suit and shoes. There were shirts, shorts, pants, socks, and underwear all neatly folded and piled in the suitcase. The shirts were a little stiff from lack of wear, but all in all he liked the clothes. There was a pair of new Nike tennis shoes still in the box at the bottom of the suitcase. He was excited to have all new clothes. He just hoped they fit.

"Well, don't you look nice," Aunt Jo said in her kind drawl as Ian stepped out on the porch with all-new clothes and shoes. He tugged at the white cotton collared shirt. It was new and a little itchy still but much better than the suit and tie he had just been freed from.

"Everything fit OK?" Aunt Jo asked.

"Yes'm," Ian answered.

"Good. I just had to guess on your size. Got some of the shorts with elastic so you'd have room to grow. Then I talked to Fred down at the department store. Gave him your approximate height and weight and such, and he helped me put together the rest. The shoes are what I'm most worried about. We can exchange 'em for another size if you'll tell me now before you scuff 'em up."

"They're fine," Ian said, embarrassed that he'd caused his aunt to fret over him so. The shoes were a little big, but he didn't want to say anything. "Uh, thanks." Ian was sincerely grateful for everything she'd done so far.

The two sat on the porch swing silently for a while enjoying the cookies and lemonade she had made for them. Ian had a lot of questions, but he really didn't want to know the answers. He was afraid then that his aunt would start asking him what he remembered about that night. He would have to tell her that he didn't remember much at all. Just the smell of smoke, the blaze, and then the flashing lights of the fire truck. Before that or even after that, he just wasn't sure about. The afternoon breeze gently pushed the swing. *Swing, swing, swing on the swing/Up so high we'll touch the sky.*

Ian managed to slip out the back door while Aunt Jo was fixing supper. The outdoor shed proved to be too much of a curiosity for him. Making sure that his aunt couldn't see him from the kitchen window, he stood in front of the double-chained doors and realized that the chain was loose. He discovered that by pulling on one of the handles his skinny body could easily slip through. All he had to do was slide through under the chain, and he was in.

It was dark inside. A little bit of sunlight came through a dirty window at the back of the shed. It was enough light to see that there was an old metal boat sitting on the floor. It looked like there were fishing poles, rods, and tackle in the boat. Ian wondered if his dead uncle had been a fisherman. He guessed it was possible for Aunt Jo to like the sport, but he had never known a female to enjoy that sort of thing. On the other side of the shed was an old lawn mower. Some homemade shelves rose above it. There was a gasoline can with a rag stuck into the spout. Ian didn't dare touch it. He knew that gasoline was dangerous. Miscellaneous tools were hung between nails hammered into the wall next to the shelves. As far as he could tell, there wasn't anything that looked the least bit valuable. He wondered why his aunt had bothered to lock the shed.

Before he slithered out between the doors, Ian thought that the shed itself might have value to him later. It could be a place he could go to figure things out.

Chapter Two

A dog barking outside
woke him. But before he opened his eyes, Ian was aware of his unfamiliar surroundings. There were sheets on the bed beneath him. That was the giveaway. He was not at home. The lumpy mattress he always slept on never had sheets, much less starched ones. When he tried to go back to sleep, the rhythm of the barking made his mind begin to concoct a rhyme. *Sheets, sheets/They help you sleep/Bed, bed/Your parents are dead.* The reality of that was neither saddening nor comforting. It was just reality. Numbing, sobering reality.

He smelled something sweet and unfamiliar. And then he heard the squeak and slam of an oven door. *Aunt Jo must have cooked breakfast,* he thought. But he reckoned that he would not be invited to join her. He would probably have to make his own breakfast as usual.

"Ian," the voice was sweet and drawled. "Ian, honey, I've

got homemade cinnamon rolls fixed." *Rolls, rolls/Rolls in the bowl* . . .

He opened his eyes and saw his aunt smiling down on him. He smiled back.

"I thought I'd let you sleep a little later today," she said while she lifted the hot, frosted rolls onto a small china plate and placed them in front of him. "We'll go around to the school later and talk to the principal, and you can meet your new teacher."

"New teacher?" Ian said, taking a bite before she could change her mind and take the breakfast away.

"Yes. We have to start you in school now that you're going to live here in Crestview," Jo said gently. "I know there's only another three weeks or so of school left before the summer, but we've got to get you registered somewhere. The school here is nice. I think you'll like it."

Ian shrugged and took another bite even before he'd swallowed the last one.

Jo's wrinkled hand touched his arm. "Now I know this will be hard for you, hon, moving in like this with your aunt Jo, somebody you hardly know."

Aunt Jo/I hardly know. It became the rhythm pattern for his chewing.

"But we'll make it, you and me. You don't have to worry." The words were sincere; the food was sweet. He savored the moment.

The school building was old and severe. It had been re-modeled on the inside to meet modern educational standards, but on the outside the school did not make Ian feel welcome at all. In fact, the sight of it was frightening. The columns out front were large and solid. The double doors were heavy. From a distance, the building resembled a lion.

The rust-colored brick was its head, the jagged shingles on the roof its mane, and the steps up into the front entrance its teeth. Eyes made of thick window glass stared at him, following him out of Aunt Jo's car and to the sidewalk. Suddenly Ian wanted to go back to his old school and, surprisingly, to his old house, the house that had burned down. As he approached the front steps, the sweet breakfast began to turn sour in his stomach. Aunt Jo gave him a gentle push when he hesitated. *Lions roar/At the door.*

"Well, Edward . . ." The principal extended his hand.

"It's Ian," Aunt Jo corrected him. "His first name is Edward, but we call him by his middle name, Ian."

Ian was struck by the "we" part. Before the fire, he couldn't think of a time that Aunt Jo had called him anything except once in the birthday card. He couldn't think if he'd ever even met her before the funeral.

The principal looked over Ian's file. Ian's stomach churned.

"Well, son, you're a good student according to this. Your teachers from your old school had nice things to say about you too." The principal smiled and raised one eyebrow.

Ian didn't know how to respond. Should he say, "thank you"? Should he say, "I know"? He needed a rhyme, he thought, but nothing came. He just nodded instead.

The school yard filled quickly when the afternoon recess bell rang. The swings and the merry-go-round were the first things to be engulfed with children. Ian leaned against the brick building and watched the swings. He loved to swing. There was rhythm there. As soon as one swinger left, another would take the vacancy quickly, and Ian didn't feel comfortable jumping in too fast. After all, this was his first day in a new school.

"Hey!"

Ian turned to see a freckle-faced boy about his size holding a red rubber ball. "Wanna play kickball?" the boy asked.

Ian shook his head. The boy shrugged, turned, and ran off.

"Tell me, hon. What do you want for supper?" Aunt Jo asked Ian as soon as he stepped off the school bus.

"Doesn't matter," Ian mumbled. His usual fare had been canned soup or rice. He could make those easily. The instructions had been easy to read.

"Well, I'll pop a roast in the oven and make potatoes and beans. You like potatoes?" she asked.

"Yes'm," Ian lied. The instant potatoes he'd fixed for himself many times were grainy or soupy or mealy or something. But he didn't want to hurt Aunt Jo's feelings. Maybe she'd cook them better than he could. Maybe she knew how to make instant potatoes taste good.

Ian heard her call him from the back stoop for supper. He waited for a second to let her go inside so he could slip out of the shed. He slid out quickly between the doors and noticed through the thick pecan trees that the sun was getting low. He didn't know for a fact that his aunt minded his going in the shed. But since there was a chain on the door, he figured she had intended to keep people out. He had been in there awhile, he guessed, just sitting in the boat pretending to float away, like in the Robert Louis Stevenson poem he loved so much.

Later, after supper, the voices in the "front room," as Aunt Jo called, it were subdued. Ian listened from his new bedroom, but he couldn't quite make out all the words. A few times, though, he heard his own name. *Ian, Ian/What you seein'?* He went around the room and rhymed every item he saw. *Books, books/Makes you look. Tick tock/I see a clock.* The voices got a little louder.

"No, Mr. Benson, he's not ready, I'm telling you." Ian didn't know anybody named Mr. Benson, and he couldn't imagine why the man was talking to Aunt Jo. He'd never heard Aunt Jo raise her voice; but then again he'd only just met Aunt Jo, so who knew what she'd do? *Knew/Do.* This thought sent his mind around the room in a rhyme again.

The front door slammed, and Ian knew he had to get back to his spelling words. Making sentences with spelling words was about the only part of homework Ian liked. His old teacher in Madison had said that he was very creative. He liked that word *creative,* even though he didn't know what it meant really. His teacher would also say that he had a good mind. He figured that being creative was having a good mind.

When the door squeaked, he looked up at Aunt Jo. She looked a little pale and serious. She started to speak, but instead she crossed the room, rubbed Ian's back, and looked over his shoulder at the books and notebook paper on the desk. She smiled sadly and then left the room.

Josephine Camellia Jones Anderson, otherwise known as Jo, had lived in Crestview all of her life. She had been born there, raised there, and married there. The older of two girls, Jo had doted on her younger sister, insisting on feeding and dressing her. Estelle, "Essie," was Jo's little doll.

A distinction between the girls soon became apparent. Essie was the Pretty One. Jo was the Good One. Essie silently reveled in the fact that she got regular calls from young boys and older men in town and Jo did not. Essie often coyly arranged blind dates for Jo with attractive young suitors of her own as a way to taunt them when they first met her homely sister. Essie loved it! Even Jo could see the disappointment in their faces when they saw her for the first time. Once, however, the disappointment didn't look so bad when Essie fixed Harlan Anderson up with her sister. Harlan was quiet, moderately handsome, and a good dancer. He and Jo danced every dance at the Methodist social that night. A year later, they were married.

Essie's child, Mary, was born out of wedlock the following year. And though times didn't really permit it, she kept the child and tried to raise her. Essie and Jo's parents were embarrassed by the child's presence, and the father, whoever he was, chose to stay at a distance. So Jo stepped in often and took Mary, doting on her just as she had Essie.

It was not hard to love Mary. She was a beautiful and happy child with engaging blue eyes. Her blonde, silky hair curved around the nape of her neck, and Jo loved to kiss her there.

Jo and Harlan remained childless themselves, but Mary became such a part of their lives that the barrenness was much easier to handle through the years. Essie died when Mary was a teenager, and so Mary lived with Jo and Harlan until she graduated from high school. By that time, however, Mary, who was more beautiful than her mother had been, had turned out to be as vain and uncaring, and bitter about her past. After Mary married Ed, she had no other contact with Aunt Jo. And then there was Ian. And next came the alcohol.

"Why don't you just forget about that girl, Josephine? She doesn't care about you. She doesn't even care about herself or that little young'n of hers," Harlan would say every time Jo wrote letters to her niece. More often than not, Jo would sneak a ten-dollar bill in the letter when Harlan wasn't watching.

When she had heard about Ian's birth, Jo had sent a nice layette ensemble for the baby. She had marked October 23 on her calendar, and every year she sent a card addressed to Master Ian Lane with money inside. There was never a thank-you or acknowledgment, but the packages and cards were never sent back either. Jo was sure that Mary had gotten each one of them. Maybe she had spent the money on Ian. Maybe not.

Chapter Three

Ian couldn't wait

to tell Aunt Jo about kickball. It had been exactly five days since he came to Crestview, and already he had made a friend and that day had kicked an infield home run!

When Aunt Jo didn't meet him at the bus stop as she had all week, Ian just figured that she was letting him assume some responsibility by walking the block home alone. But there was more to her absence.

In the driveway was a black car. Ian didn't recognize it. Of course, the only cars he would recognize would have been Aunt Jo's Chevy, his father's clunker, and Nick's or Trooper's beat-up trucks. This car was none of those. It looked newer and more official.

Ian found Aunt Jo in the front room talking to a man, younger than Aunt Jo, about his father's age, he guessed.

"Ian, hon, this is Mr. Frank Benson from over in Madison. Do you ever remember seeing him?" Jo asked.

Ian shook his head. He thought this might be the same

Mr. Benson who had been in the front room a few nights before.

"I don't think we ever met, did we, son?" The man tried to be cordial, but Ian was skeptical and held back. He stood behind the couch where Aunt Jo sat.

Ian shook his head again.

"There's some cookies, homemade, laying out on a towel to cool, hon. Why don't you go and test them out?" Ian suspected this might be Aunt Jo's way of getting him out of the room so she and the stranger could talk more. It was OK. He didn't care to talk to the stranger anymore, and the cookies smelled like heaven.

Ian shuffled his feet and disappeared behind the swinging door to the kitchen.

The conversation was serious. *Adults always talk low when there's something wrong or serious to talk about,* he thought. Munching on a sugar cookie, Ian tried to listen.

"Fire . . . evidence . . . careless . . . the boy . . ." Those were the only words Ian could make out. By her tone, it seemed that Aunt Jo was arguing some of the particulars surrounding the stranger's comments. Suddenly the sweet taste of the cookie became bitter in Ian's mouth. *Fire, fire/It just gets higher/Flame, flame/I'm to blame./Shame! Shame!/I'm to blame!* What was happening? he wondered. Was this man a policeman come to arrest him? Frank didn't wear a uniform, but on TV he'd seen plainclothes cops with badges in their pockets. Was this man a social worker come to take him away? He'd seen that on TV too. Was Aunt Jo his protector, or was she in cahoots with Mr. Benson? He thought she was being a little too nice. What were they arguing about? He didn't wait to find out.

He was careful not to slam the back door. He first thought of the shed behind the house as a place to hide, but it would only be a temporary refuge. He stopped to think, but only for a moment, to let his mind catch up with his heart rate.

Ian dashed down the lanes that separated the clapboard houses from each other. A box van with a delivery service name on it was coming from his left. It slowed down to make the turn onto a main street. Ian slowed down too, not wanting to raise suspicion and cause the driver to recognize him as a boy on the run.

The brakes squealed. The truck stopped on a slight grade to let another car pass.

Ian saw the back door loose on the van. He climbed on the lip of the van, reached up, and pushed up on the handle with all his strength. The truck rolled backwards slightly and Ian inhaled exhaust fumes, but the sting in his lungs somehow empowered him to climb inside the van, closing the door behind him.

He gasped for air, lay down on the van's empty floor, and thought about what he was about to do.

He couldn't tell whether it was day or night. The van's cargo area had no windows. He knew he'd been asleep, but he couldn't tell how long.

Voices and sounds outside told him that they were at a gas station. Ian could hear the rattle of the pump handle being lifted and the roar of the gasoline filling the tank. Somebody was talking—two men—about fishing. One had caught a nice string of bass in the river. The other hadn't had a nibble all day at the lake. Each vowed to the other that they'd go together to the river that weekend. There were some thank-yous, and Ian assumed the transaction of money for gas was complete.

Ian suddenly had a bad thought. He hoped this truck

wasn't going to Madison. That's all he needed now, to go back home right into the arms of the law. But there was no way Ian could tell which direction they were traveling or how close or how far they were from his own fate.

His dark confines and the rumble of the van rocked him to sleep again.

This time, he didn't hear voices or sounds. He just awoke and realized that the van had stopped. He listened carefully, putting his ear against the wall of the van. There didn't seem to be anyone around. Slowly he felt his way to the door and lifted the handle slightly. It was as dark outside as it was inside. He raised the door a little more and peered out into the night.

The smell was of garbage. Ian knew he was either near a Dumpster or in an alley. He looked down to see how far off the ground he actually was standing. Trying to judge that kind of thing in the dark could be tricky. Using his best guess, he jumped flat-footed to the hard surface. It was an alley. It was near a Dumpster. It was also as quiet as a tomb. Making his way to the street wasn't so hard. He followed the light coming from a shop on the corner. But instead of just presenting himself in full to the scene, he hugged the wall, inched his way along it, and slowly peered around the corner.

The street was deserted. The shop's lights were just for security, because Ian couldn't see anybody inside.

It must be the middle of the night, Ian thought. None of the other businesses was open either. The shop looked like a café or bakery. Ian remembered the cookies on Aunt Jo's counter. He wished he had taken several of them with him before he had run away.

Ian was relieved when he realized that he wasn't in Madison or Crestview. This town was a little too big for either one of those places. Ian guessed this would be like a city. The downtown section looked like it went beyond his eyesight. It smelled different too, like more people generally used this space. There was another odor that he could not identify at first. Fish, maybe. Wet litter lay in the runoff gutters. Ian suddenly felt sticky all over.

He sat on the curb and thought. First, he thought about Aunt Jo. Maybe he shouldn't be so suspicious. Maybe he should just forget about her. She hadn't had time to get to know him anyway. And who's to say she intended to? Then he thought about the stranger. Ian had already surmised that the stranger was not out for his good.

Then Ian thought about his parents. Most of his early memories of them were blurred. The only vivid remembrances were of his dad swearing at the mailman for not delivering his disability check. Or of his mom burning her hand on the skillet and then flinging the skillet with hot grease across the kitchen. It was then that Ian decided it was time to bring in the mail and to cook all the meals. He figured that he would save the mailman from having to hear such foul language. He decided he could take it himself. At least he was used to it.

The decision to take over the cooking was as much for self-preservation as it was for the common good. Ian didn't know when the frying pan of grease was going to be hurled at him. He took a safer route. He would take small amounts of cash from his dad's wallet or from his mother's purse every other day or so. When he had enough, he would stop by the grocery store and pick up easy-fix meals. He could read instructions and he could boil water. How hard could it be? He'd fix macaroni and cheese or canned ravioli in a small saucepan. Most of the time, he ate all he wanted alone and left the rest on the stove for whenever his parents woke up. Almost every morning, Ian would find the pan empty. Then in the afternoon, he would wash the pan and start over with another dish.

The day that Aunt Jo's birthday card had come, he had felt adventurous and tried to bake a cake from a mix, but it didn't get done enough. He ate some of the sweet, gooey batter, leaving the rest on the counter. The next morning the batter was gone.

He had cooked for himself, and for his parents, every day for a year. He had learned so much, like how long to boil rice and what not to put in a microwave. Although these were things that most kids knew, his experiences had taught him much more. He could tell when spaghetti was done, when strawberries were in season, and when chicken was at a good price. That was certainly more than most ten-year-old boys knew.

Another light came on in the bakery. It startled Ian, and he jumped up and backed against the alley wall. Finally, he peered around the corner into the window to see what looked like the owner getting ready for another day of business. The clock on the wall said five o'clock. That was obviously five in the morning. Forgetting himself for a second, he gaped at the pastries the man was putting in the display case. Ian's empty stomach hurt. He'd left his backpack in Aunt Jo's kitchen. He had no money at all to buy food. Ian wondered if the man might have pity on him and give him a little taste of something. But then he decided it was too risky. What if the man called the police or Aunt Jo? Ian would go to jail for his crime.

Something moved in the alley behind him. Ian quickly slid down the wall and into a tight ball, looking through the darkness to see who or what it was. *Dark, dark . . .* "What rhymes with dark?" Ian asked himself softly. His heart beat faster and he drew his knees even closer to him. *Dark, dark. . . .* He heard it move again. *Dark, dark/An angry shark!* He half-smiled. *Yes!* he thought.

Just then a door leading to the other side of the alley opened. A dim light peeked out, and Ian could see a cat race to it and disappear inside.

A cat! Ian felt a little silly for his fear. But in his situation, he couldn't be too careful.

Wait a minute, he thought. *Wonder where that door goes?* Slowly he moved to the other wall, carefully hugging it and then inching himself down it toward the door.

He listened quietly and could hear a muffled man's voice and then a meow of the cat. The conversation between man and beast lingered for a while and then faded away from him. When he could hear them no more, Ian reached for the doorknob. Slowly he tried to turn it. It would not turn at all. It was locked. But when he pushed it slightly away from him, the door opened. Apparently the lock had been set, but whoever opened it last had not closed the door completely. He was inside!

Ian discovered that the dim light he had seen before was coming from above a sink, a kitchen sink. A kitchen! That meant food! It didn't look like a restaurant. It was too small, for one thing, and the appliances looked more like those you'd find in a home. But it didn't look like a home kitchen either, more industrial. To his left there were four small tables and some folding chairs. To his right were the sink, a stove, and a refrigerator. Ian only imagined what would be kept in the refrigerator.

Ian was afraid that whoever had let the cat in probably was still in the building, so he stood for several minutes listening for sounds. After not hearing voices or movement of any kind, he looked down at his own feet to make sure there

31

was nothing in front of him that would cause a noise if he took a step or two. He moved closer and closer to the refrigerator. Just as he reached it, he heard footsteps coming downstairs to his left. He didn't want to panic; he just wanted to hide quickly. He was too far away from the door to exit into the alley in time, so he grabbed at a doorknob to the left of the refrigerator. It opened, and Ian stepped through and quickly closed the door behind him. Everything went dark again. He must have been inside a closet of some kind, but he didn't dare reach to either side of him for fear he'd knock something off a shelf.

Steps grew closer and closer. Ian stuck one foot behind him, carefully feeling to see what was there. He took a step back farther into the closet. It sounded as if the footsteps stopped right in front of the closet door! He retreated again, taking another small step back. Then there was humming. The man, maybe the one who had let the cat in, was humming, and the sound was very close, right outside the closet door. Then there was more light coming from under the closet door.

Next Ian heard some banging and clanging of utensils, then water running, and then a faint industrial hum. Ian figured the man was making coffee. Then he heard the refrigerator door open, some rattling like glass bottles hitting together, a little more humming, more rattling, then pouring, then the refrigerator door closing. The humming continued, but in between gulps and chewing.

"Not bad for day-old doughnuts," mumbled the man. Ian was so hungry he almost burst through the closet door to grab the last morsels before the man ate them, but he kept calm. He tried to create a rhyme to go with the man's humming, but the tune was indistinguishable and the rhythm was disjointed, so Ian just closed his eyes and tried to block out his hunger in another way. The smell of the brewing coffee was starting to fill the room too, and Ian thought of the many mornings he had brewed coffee for his parents before they woke up. He knew they would drink it to help with the hangovers they always had.

A dull knock came from somewhere above his head. Ian could hear the man shuffling slightly; then there were footsteps going up the stairs. He could bear it no more. Quickly Ian opened the closet door, and he spotted a partially eaten doughnut and a half-empty glass of milk on the counter beside the sink. Tearing off part of the doughnut and stuffing it into his mouth, then taking one long gulp of milk from the glass, Ian was in and out of the closet in under fifteen seconds. It had to be a record. He didn't want to take any chances of the man seeing him or knowing he was there. But before he closed the door, he could see that the closet was a pantry, filled with canned goods and staples of all kinds. He almost collapsed with relief!

For a minute or two, the muffled voices of two men hovered above his head. Ian figured that one of the men was the man whose doughnut and milk he had just swiped. But the other he couldn't imagine and couldn't care less about. He had a thought, though. Maybe he'd have time to take another bite and another sip, or maybe even time to rummage through the refrigerator himself. As long as the men were upstairs having a conversation, he could have a few minutes to explore the kitchen.

When he opened the pantry door slightly, he could see almost everything in it. Up high were large cans: tomatoes, corn. On the middle shelves were dried beans, rice, and bags of uncooked pasta. On the lower shelves were more canned goods and some paper products.

Suddenly, a cat appeared at the door, peering in, curious

to what was behind the door. "Meow," the cat called. And before Ian knew it, the cat had slipped through the open door.

"Go away, kitty. Shoo!" Ian whispered. But instead of that making the cat disappear, another cat slipped in behind it. "Oh, no, shoo! Shoo, cats!" Ian turned the cats around and ushered them quickly out the door, only to have them crawl over each other to return.

"No! Hey, is this where they keep your food, kitties?" Ian figured that as soon as the man returned he'd open the pantry to get the cat food and find him hiding. He promised himself not to panic. He thought quickly. Opening the pantry door, he ushered the cats out first, then walked out himself, closing the door behind him. He took a doughnut morsel and enticed the cats to the floor in front of the sink. While they ate, Ian searched quickly for another place to hide. Across the dining area, he saw two doors. One said "Ladies," the other "Men." Figuring he'd have a better chance right then of going undetected in the ladies' room, he stepped inside just in time. He heard the man's footsteps coming down the stairs.

"Hey, get down off'a there, Mercy! You too, Hope." The man good-naturedly shooed the cats down off the counter. Apparently the cats had jumped to the counter in search of more food. "Hey, wait a minute," the man spoke to the meowing cats. "Which one of you scoundrels nibbled on my doughnut and drank my milk when I wasn't looking?"

It was a little humiliating to hide out in a ladies' powder room, but Ian figured that the man wouldn't find him there, and the cats would have no reason to want to get in that room. He listened for a while. The man was pouring himself a cup of coffee and another glass of milk and pulling another doughnut out of a bag. The cats meowed.

"No, girls, no doughnuts for you. You get the good stuff." Ian could hear the man open the pantry. He was glad he had gotten out of there.

"Here ya go." Ian heard dry cat food spilling into a bowl. The man then apparently sat down at one of the tables and drank his coffee and leisurely read the morning paper. Ian thought he'd never leave.

Daylight came through an opaque bathroom window. Ian waited. Finally, the man walked up the stairs, all the while talking to the cats, who meowed affectionately. Then the building was quiet for a long time. It was probably an hour after that when Ian got the courage to venture out. The place seemed to be abandoned, for he couldn't even hear the cats anymore. Ian explored the kitchen first. The pantry had only staples as he had suspected. He knew he could cook the rice if he had to, but he'd rather not. Something ready to eat would be better. He finally found some stale crackers and jugs of watered-down juice in one of the cabinets. He ate a few crackers from a couple of boxes and drank some of the juice from a tiny cup, but he was careful not to leave crumbs or to take so much that it would be missed.

The kitchen area looked a little homier than he had first thought. The tables had small arrangements of fake flowers on them. Some folding chairs were placed around the tables. The rest were stacked in a corner. The room was stark but very clean, and there was a collage of pictures on a bulletin board on one wall. The pictures were of children playing basketball, old people in wheelchairs opening packages, and one picture of some people singing around a man with a guitar. Ian wondered if the man with the guitar was the man that he had almost encountered. The only windows in the kitchen were high at the top of the walls, and from what he could see through them, they looked out just above ground level. Ian figured that this kitchen was in the basement of a larger building.

There were rooms adjacent to the kitchen. Making sure no one was close by, he continued his tour. A couple of the rooms were lined with little chairs. There were pictures hanging low on the walls, pictures that were paintings of ancient figures. The figures wore robes and costumes with headpieces and had sandals on their feet. The men had long hair, and one man seemed to be in several of the pictures, and he was usually the center of attention. Children in ancient costumes gathered around with flowers in their hands. In one picture the main man was touching a girl who looked sick. Finally, Ian found a picture that looked a little familiar. This one was of a man and woman gathered around a wooden box lined with hay. There was a chubby, fair-haired little baby lying on the hay with his hands up. A tiny halo encircled his head. Ian remembered that this was part of the Christmas story. There had been a scene similar to this on the lawn of a church in Madison. Somebody had called it a nativity scene.

The place was as quiet as a tomb. Occasionally, Ian would hear some foot traffic outside, but no sound that he could tell came from inside the building.

The stairs led up to another level. Carefully he climbed them, stopping every step or two to listen for the presence of others.

The steps opened up into a long, thin room. The carpet was a dirty burgundy and quite well worn. There was a large table with intricate symbols carved into it. Some papers and a nice dried flower arrangement sat on the table. Two very large wooden doors, much larger than the ones to Aunt Jo's shed, were opposite the table. Ian figured that they went outside the building. He pushed on the right-hand door and it wouldn't budge. The left one wouldn't open either. Then he saw that they were locked with a dead bolt.

His hunger was too great for him to explore further. He had to return to the kitchen to try to find something else to eat.

Chapter Four

The Madison Police

Department had done all it could do. Several uniformed officers and one investigator had searched everywhere for the boy. The officials were beginning to conclude that Ian Lane had not returned to his hometown, at least not yet. The police in Crestview, however, were still looking high and low for him. They had found one witness who said he had seen a boy that fit Ian's description running down a side street on Friday afternoon. The witness had seen Ian crawl into the back of a white box van but couldn't remember a license plate or any other distinguishing properties of the van. Local police officials immediately put Ian's picture and information on the state's Missing Children Information Clearinghouse website. His face would be on TV news in a hundred-mile radius. There was no evidence of abduction, so an Amber Alert was not issued for the boy. Everything else that a law enforcement official could do was done. But the most promising element of the search process was Josephine Anderson. She would see to it that no one rested until Ian Lane was found.

"Keep looking!" Jo demanded for the tenth time. She had been to the sheriff's office at least five times in the past eighteen hours.

"Miz Anderson, we've got people lookin' for that boy from the 'Bama line down to the bay. We talked to the Amtrak people, and no little boy has traveled unaccompanied in either direction," the sheriff said.

"Maybe he's hitchhiked somewhere," Jo continued. "Anything else on that van they think he jumped in?"

"No, ma'am, and we've checked with dispatchers and talked with truckers on CB. So far, not a soul has spotted 'im. We personally called every county sheriff's office in the Panhandle too, and nobody's seen hide nor hair."

"Well, keep looking. He couldn't have gotten far, and he couldn't have vanished into thin air. He's just been missing since yesterday." Jo was on the verge of tears.

"I know, ma'am. A little feller like that couldn'ta got more'n a few miles in that length of time. Our next step might be to drag the river."

"No! Don't say that!" Finally Jo burst into tears.

"I know you don't like to think about it, ma'am, that some kinda harm coulda come to the boy, but we've gotta turn over every rock, ya know," the sheriff explained.

"Then turn over every rock, every leaf, every blade of grass!" Jo yelled indignantly and stood to exit. "And don't leave one stone unturned!"

The outburst was uncharacteristic of Jo Anderson. She was known as a true lady, a saint in the hamlet of Crestview. Most everybody knew how she had loved her sister, Essie, and little Mary. No one was surprised when Jo offered to take Ian into her home and raise him. It was just the way Jo was, always opening her home to somebody.

The fact that Jo was a good cook was the best-known fact in the county. Her pies and her cakes were the marvel of the Panhandle. She had won cook-offs and recipe contests galore. She had even won a $1,000 prize from *Southern Living* magazine for her peanut butter bonbons, a confection that was a variation on another recipe, but this version was uniquely hers.

Young soldiers from Eglin Air Force Base, boys away from home for the first time, knew after their first day there about Jo Anderson and her cooking. She was a legend that the airmen passed along to the new guys on post. Jo would host the newcomers every other month in the church's kitchen. It was her ministry and an outreach that the church heartily endorsed. While Harlan was alive, many a serviceman would find himself housed at "Andersons' Arms" as Harlan jokingly called it. Every holiday, boys who couldn't get home could come to Harlan and Jo's for dinner. Her chicken and dumplings were her signature entrée, and it seemed no matter how much she cooked, it would be gone before she knew it. Harlan had learned to overfill his plate the first time. Otherwise he wouldn't get seconds.

Frank Benson had been in the insurance business all of his adult life. His father and his uncle had been in the business before him. They had sold insurance . . . life, health, car . . . but had also sold real estate. In Madison, not much real estate business presented itself, but whatever there was the Benson Brothers got it. And that's how they made their fortune.

When Frank joined the business, his father and uncle

were old and quite sedate and had just been waiting until Frank was old enough to take it over. They practically gave the company to the younger Benson, whom they trained well, but they'd occasionally stop by the office to offer advice or to handle an old account. Some old clients insisted on the services of the older generation, being a little leery of Frank's inexperience. Frank made a name for himself, though, as a good businessman, and before long the old brothers spent all their time fishing on Lake Seminole or watching the Gators play football in the Swamp. It was then that Frank decided to drop the real estate business and concentrate on insurance.

The Madison Volunteer Fire Department was surprisingly dedicated. But they weren't completely volunteers either. Each of the four men received a small stipend for his services. One of only a few millionaires in Madison County had set up a fund for it a few years before, after the department put out a fire at one of his farm equipment warehouses. All the men were "homeboys," meaning they were born and raised in the county and probably would have done the job without pay. Each of them had other jobs, of course, but their employers were glad to let them have swing schedules to accommodate "the duty."

One of the volunteers was Walter Patton, who divided his time between being a city policeman and a fireman. He and Andy McFay had been first on the scene at the Lane house. They had found it fully engaged with victims still inside. There was no way they could have gotten in. The heat was intense, and they could hear a woman and a man screaming. Frantically, Walter and Andy had searched for a way in or out. Before they could reach the victims, the roof had collapsed and the fire had been completely out of control. They hadn't heard the screams anymore, just the roar of the blaze. The water truck had only kept it from spreading to the other houses. They had been able finally to contain it to the immediate property. That's when Walter had found Ian, sitting in his underwear beside a crepe myrtle bush at the edge of the yard. The boy stared into the blaze, but he had been mumbling something that Walter could not identify. It had sounded like a limerick.

"What do y'all reckon 'bout that fire, Frank?" Felix Newberry asked from the other side of the coffee shop counter as he served up Frank's first cup. The Saturday coffee crowd hadn't arrived yet.

"I don't know anything yet, Felix. The great-aunt won't let me talk to the boy, and the state fire marshal hasn't finished his report yet," Frank answered. "It'll be awhile yet before we know anything."

Just then the rest of crowd began to dribble in. First in was the bank president, next was the preacher, and finally, completing the crowd, was Walter. Instead of taking a seat on a stool at the counter, Walter leaned over Frank's shoulder.

"I need to talk to you for a second," Walter said, keeping his voice down.

"Shoot." Frank wondered what Walter had on his mind.

"Nah, outside," Walter said seriously. Frank followed him out the door.

On the street, Walter told Frank about the report regarding the disappearance of Ian Lane.

Jo jumped up to answer the door.

"Oh, glory!" she cried with excitement. She was distressed to find Frank Benson from Madison on her doorstep instead of Ian.

"Have you heard from Ian yet?" asked Frank.

"No," Jo said tersely.

"You must be worried sick."

"Yes."

"Is there anything I can do?" Frank sounded truly concerned.

"No, you've done enough, Mr. Benson." Jo tried to be polite, but it was difficult.

"Missus Anderson, you have to understand that I was just doing my job, trying to investigate this fire. I had no intentions of scaring the boy."

"I'm sure you didn't, but that doesn't help right now, does it? Ian is gone. He must've overheard you talking about the fire. Now . . . poor boy." And the tears began to flow again.

Ian's stomach growled. For the first time that day, Ian thought about Aunt Jo. He figured she had discovered he was missing by then, but he didn't think she would really care that much. Maybe she would leave food on the counter for him in case he came home, but he wasn't too concerned. He even figured she might be relieved to not have him around.

He stood in front of the basement refrigerator for a while, letting the coldness make chills come up on his arms. The milk carton was almost full. He figured he could get away with one glass full without the man missing it. There were also several plastic containers stacked neatly on the middle shelf. One at a time, Ian peeled back the tops of the containers. Most of them seemed to contain combinations of several foods thrown together. One had macaroni and ground beef mixed. Another had a green glob that might have had marshmallows mixed in. Another had peas and asparagus in a rather odd-looking grayish concoction. These were obviously leftovers. Ian had no idea what they were or how long they had been left over. But he took a spoonful of each and swallowed almost without tasting. It was a trick he had learned after he started cooking his own meals.

The food went down and made his stomach cold on the inside. He wished for a cup of hot coffee to wash it down. Instead, he washed the spoon and the glass in the sink and carefully placed them back where he found them.

Now what? Maybe he would explore some more.

Listening again for noises above him, Ian climbed the stairs again, back to the long narrow room where he had ended his tour before. *There's got to be more to this building,* he thought.

The burgundy carpet from the room seemed to continue under the doors to his left. He decided to follow it. He pushed against the door nearest to him, and when he entered the room, it was an amazing discovery. It was a large room, about the size of the auditorium at his new school, he thought. There were large benches lined neatly on either side of him. He walked slowly past the rows, noticing that each bench had a sort of bookshelf with two or three old books stuck in it.

Ahead of him was a raised stage with a large stand in the middle. On the floor in front of the stage was an old but very elegant table. There were words inscribed on it. "Do This in Remembrance of Me," Ian read aloud, catching himself and looking around to make sure no one had heard him.

Though he had never been inside one, Ian was beginning to realize where he might be. There was another clue, however, that made it clearer. On the large table was an open book. A Bible, he was pretty sure, was the book on display.

Chapter Five

Reverend Jim Copeland

was doing what he always did on Saturday afternoons. He went door to door. His once-new map of Greater
Mobile was already tattered, circled, and tired, and he'd
only been at Broad Street less than a year. As he often did
while working too hard to revive the old inner-city church,
he thought back to the agonizing soul search that had
brought him to Broad Street.

"I don't think God wants me at a traditional first-church-
out-of-seminary church, Abbie. A county seat or a country
church sounds like it would be too comfortable," Jim had
said just days before his graduation from New Orleans Seminary. All of the preaching students were being "turned out,"
as they called it, into the world to baptize and make disciples,
like the Great Commission commanded. The other guys
seemed to be looking for churches with healthy growth po-
tential. But Jim's direction was still unclear.

Three churches had talked to Jim about his becoming

their pastor. He prayerfully considered each one. The first was his part-time seminary church, a sweet little congregation out in the Louisiana countryside. They had been so kind to Jim and Abbie in their two years there. Because they couldn't pay the pastor a large salary, they made up for it by giving him fresh vegetables from their gardens, jars of jellies and preserves, and sides of beef at slaughter time. The standard joke was: "You may be poor, but you'll never go hungry here." Their offer was for a full-time pastorate, but the salary couldn't reflect the extra hours.

The second church that contacted the young Brother Copeland was a church in the Mississippi Delta. It was a county-seat town, and the church was of good size. The people were very kind, the town was family oriented, the salary was good, and they provided a comfortable pastorium. For a while, this seemed like the best choice. Still Jim wasn't sure this was where God wanted him.

The third church was Broad Street. Its location was deplorable, the salary was worse, and the benefits were almost nonexistent. It had once been a thriving church built in the Gilded Age of the early 1920s. The city itself had had a lot of growth from industry, and it seemed to be attracting new people all the time. Then, as time went by, the city population moved to the sprawl of the suburbs. The Broad Street area was left to urban decline. But the church answered the attrition with an aggressive bus ministry, and for a decade the church brought in children and families left behind in the city. However, when the busing trend went out of style, a remnant tried to hang on by catering to an older loyal generation and to the inner city. In what some said was an act of faith and others called desperation, the membership of 120, mostly elderly, decided to remain at the location. They voted to extend a call to a young, energetic pastor, hoping that he could help them attract more members.

Abbie had been with Jim through sleepless nights while he wrestled with the Almighty, just like Jacob did in the Old Testament. He did this every time there was a big decision to make. Jim would stay up night after night, praying, talking it out with God and often with her. Patience, she'd tell herself. Patience and submission.

The decision to answer the call to Broad Street was particularly tiring. Each night Jim would retreat into prayer, and he'd come back and tell Abbie in the morning that he found no logical reason to accept the job. And then he would say how he couldn't get the church out of his mind. In fact, his heart broke every time he dismissed the possibility.

Finally, one morning, Abbie woke up to find Jim sitting next to the bed. He was smiling at her as she forced her eyes to open.

"Broad Street. I don't know why, but that's where God wants me, Abbie. I've just prayed that He'll reveal to me my purpose there." And with that, he crawled under the covers next to her and slept deeply for hours.

The summers in south Alabama were as unbearable as in New Orleans. Humidity and heat together with the enormous gnat population made a miserable combination. It was only May, and already Abbie was dreading the next few months, especially now that she was pregnant. She swatted a gnat, sipped on a glass of ice water, and inspected her ankles for swelling. She wondered if she'd make it to her due date, the first of August.

Jim hadn't let her go visiting with him for the last couple of months. The swelling in her ankles seemed to get worse when she walked, and besides that she looked so uncomfortable. Abbie looked big from her third month. The doctor had sworn that she was carrying a single child and ultrasound had confirmed it, but Jim wasn't so sure. Her belly was already so large that she looked like she might explode. And she had three months to go!

Jim prayed silently for Abbie and the baby, wiped the sweat off his brow, and knocked on the door of another dingy apartment.

Ian memorized the page number so he could make sure that the Bible was back like he found it. Then he thumbed through the ancient pages. He recognized most of the words, but some he thought might be foreign expressions. *Ezekiel. Malachi. Habakkuk.*

The book had no pictures, so he could only guess at their meaning. He couldn't even think of rhymes for those words.

Leaving the Bible on its pedestal, Ian climbed the steps to the stage. He couldn't even see over the stand. He figured that whoever spoke from there had to be a giant.

Chapter Six

J. D. Sullivan had never

seen anything like it in his twenty-five years as a mortician. He had prepared hundreds of bodies for burial, some of them in advanced states of decomposition and some mutilated in car crashes and other accidents. One was almost mummified after it was found in a cave by an explorer. It turned out to be the body of a missing man whose wife ten years before had been suspected of foul play, but there was never any evidence to convict her. The case was still open with the state bureau, but it was not an active investigation at the Madison Police Department.

The bodies of Ed and Mary Lane had been so burned that there was almost nothing to bury. Dental records had positively identified them, but their remains didn't even resemble human beings. J. D. had laid them to rest thinking it was almost a favor to the community and to the young survivor whom he did not know. J. D. didn't think that the Lanes would have had burial policies, but he found out that they had been rather well insured. Jo had inquired about how much the caskets, the plots, and the mortuary services had cost. J. D. said that he would send her a bill, but the policy paid off quickly and completely.

Jo took two Tylenol tablets for her headache. Ever since Ian's disappearance she hadn't slept or eaten. She just couldn't.

The phone rang.

"Miz Jo, you heard anything yet?" She recognized the voice of her pastor, Brother Brewton.

"No, Pastor, not a word," answered Jo dejectedly.

"We've been praying 'bout it all day. Irene's Sunday school class is on their way right now to bring you a meal. I know it's past lunchtime, but it took 'em a little while to get organized. Maybe you can heat it up for dinner."

"I appreciate it, Pastor. I haven't had any appetite, but, well, I appreciate it."

In Crestview, as in most small Southern towns, a meal was prepared for every bereavement. Food was the universal offering of condolence. However, Jo had usually been on the giving end.

The ladies arrived while Jo was still on the phone.

"Hey, hon. We brought you something," explained Irene Brewton, the pastor's wife. "Clara cooked butter beans, Eloise cooked sweet corn, and I fixed a pot roast with potatoes. Now, if you're not hungry now, we'll just put everything in the icebox and you can heat it up later. Jean Mayer is bringing a lemon pie in a little bit. She couldn't change her hair appointment this morning, so she got a late start."

Jo tried to be gracious and express her appreciation to the ladies, but she had no intention of eating, not until somebody found Ian safe and sound.

The ladies gathered around Jo and offered a prayer.

"Lord, please protect little Ian wherever he is. And, God, give Miz Jo here the peace that passeth understanding."

Jo felt suddenly weak in the knees before the ladies got to their amens. They helped Jo to the couch and finished their prayer as they propped up her head on some pillows and applied a cold compress. They all began to cry.

Abbie's first contraction came around 3:15. It wasn't really strong, and it lasted less than a minute. Then another at around 3:20. Three more came at five-minute intervals. Having been to birthing classes, she was aware that these were probably Braxton-Hicks contractions. She had expected them and wasn't particularly alarmed when they began. She did, however, lie down and elevate her legs. She wouldn't even tell Jim about them. He was out visiting in the city housing apartments, and she knew she couldn't get in touch with him anyway. Picking up the TV remote control, she tried to take her mind off the pain.

"We interrupt this program to bring you a special bulletin," said the voice from a TV station in Pensacola. "A ten-year-old orphan boy has been reported missing from his foster home in Crestview." A picture of a small boy suddenly flashed on the screen. He had shaggy blond hair and a crooked grin. "Ian Lane, whose parents died in Madison a week ago in a house fire, is missing from his great-aunt's home in Crestview. He was last seen Friday, yesterday, at approximately 3:30 P.M. He was wearing denim jeans, a light blue T-shirt, and white Nike shoes. Anyone knowing the whereabouts of this boy should contact the Florida State Police force at 1-800-555-4334."

"Poor child," Abbie said, trying to find something on the TV that was soothing and pleasant. Finally she landed on the Saturday afternoon movie. The contractions seemed to be less intense and farther apart. By the end of the movie they had stopped completely. Apparently, she dozed off for a while, because the next thing she remembered was Jim standing over her.

"What time is it?" she groggily asked her husband.

"Four thirty-ish," he said, looking at his watch and then kneeling beside the couch and taking her hand.

"Wow. I must have nodded off for a while," she said.

"You feeling OK, babe?"

"Yeah, just resting a little is all. My ankles were swelling, so I thought I'd get off my feet."

Jim smiled and clicked off the TV. He was concerned about Abbie's health. She seemed to have a lot of swelling, and sometimes her face looked flushed. She was going to the doctor every month like she was supposed to, but Jim was still worried that something wasn't right.

"How'd it go today in the housing project?" Abbie asked.

"Oh, fine. Lots of kids over there. I think we ought to do a Backyard Bible Club this summer. It may be the only way we can minister to them. There's one woman there who might be a prospect to host the club. She isn't going to a church, she said, but she told me she was a Christian. I don't know, maybe. I tried to talk to her, but her kids were crying and making such a racket, I'm not sure what I said or what she said." Jim looked tired.

"Well, sounds like a Backyard Bible Club would be a

great idea, then. I'll help you," Abbie said, rubbing her husband's hand. She could always tell when he was discouraged. She knew, of course, that Jim wouldn't let her do any such thing. The closer to her due date she came, the more he insisted that she take it easy. Mostly all he would let her do was listen and pray for him.

The ministry at Broad Street hadn't gone the way they had expected. The older membership was very loving and sincere. Many of them were great prayer warriors, but because of their age, they couldn't really do much work. All of the visiting had fallen to Jim and Abbie, but lately she couldn't go on the Saturday visits. Jim wasn't seeing any growth in membership at all. He had baptized no one in more than a year. Two deaths of members meant that his membership had actually decreased.

The afternoon had been a treasure hunt for Ian. On his tour of the church, he'd found lots of interesting things. There was a room, bigger than a closet but smaller than his bedroom at Aunt Jo's. He discovered it down a long hallway and up a short flight of stairs above the auditorium. The room was mostly empty except for some long steel pipes that stood in front of a sheer panel of cloth. Ian wondered if these were like heating ducts, some sort of large radiator. They weren't warm to the touch, but then again it was May and the heat wouldn't be on anyway. Through the pipes, Ian could look down over the stage and see all the benches in nice neat little rows. The speaker's stand didn't look quite so huge from his new vantage point. In fact, everything looked somewhat miniature to him. He figured he was up about twenty feet or so.

The room didn't look as if it was being used for anything much. The door to it was unlocked, but the hallway and stairs that led to it had old flower arrangements, a broken chair, and a stack of books lining them. Ian had to move some things out of the way just to get in the door. He figured that this room was rarely, if ever, used. He liked the place. It had a view too, like a perch in a parakeet cage. He could live unnoticed there for a while. He'd need to gather a few things, he thought, to make the place livable, but his tour wasn't over yet. It could make a nice little nest.

In the hallway leading to his new room were two doors to his right. Opening one he found it to be smaller than his room. It had no windows either, but it had a rack with a few white robes hanging on it. Next to the rack was a hook where the largest pair of galoshes he had ever seen hung. He quickly closed the door and opened the other. That's what he was looking for. A tiny bathroom with sink and toilet. Yes, he had all the comforts of home here. Well, actually, this would be more comfortable than home.

Carefully, Ian selected some food items from his original hiding place, the pantry. Apparently, he hadn't looked closely the first time. When he studied the shelves he found one marked "Lord's Supper." He figured the Lord wouldn't mind sharing His supper with a hungry child. There was a large tin with several packages of saltines in it. All but one of the packages were still sealed. He took one of the sealed ones and rearranged the others so that he could disguise the space that the one he took left behind. He also found four jars of grape juice, all unopened. He took one and hoped whoever kept up with the inventory would think that they had miscounted. And maybe he could even replace the items later before anybody noticed they were gone. In the back corner of the pantry was a shelf marked "Food Bank."

He found unopened cans of tuna, soup, vegetables, and one large jar of peanut butter. The cans and the jar had dust on the top of them. Ian figured that these had been here long enough that the people would have forgotten about them. He took a can of each item, a can opener from a kitchen drawer, and the whole jar of peanut butter. It was a risk he'd have to take.

Before dark, Ian had collected a small mattress, a pillow, and a blanket he found in a closet. He had a bed and a small stash of food. He knew he'd have to ration the food to make it go further, but he sat in his new home and had an introductory feast. Then he slept soundly.

Chapter Seven

The wet sand beneath

her feet is warm and soft, but she is running too fast to notice. The beach is full of people, and none of them is Ian. One by one she asks them if they have seen a boy, ten years old, blond hair, blue eyes. "His name is Ian," she pleads. But they all shake their heads, together, in unison.

She looks toward the water, and far out into the gulf she sees a tiny speck. The sun glares above her, and she shades her eyes.

She sees the head bobbing up and down and then going under. "Ian," she gasps.

Without thinking, she runs headlong into the surf. Her clothes get drenched, but she doesn't care. Her arms start to paddle frantically and her feet kick wildly. However, no matter how hard she swims, the distance between her and the boy widens. She swims harder, but the boy drifts farther.

She stops and looks to the horizon and begins to weep.

"No! No!" she cries. And the scene fades.

Jo sat up and looked at the clock. She had only been sleeping an hour, and this was already the second nightmare she'd had. The first one was much like the second; Ian was beyond her reach.

She sat on the edge of the bed, wiped the perspiration from her forehead with a tissue, and prayed.

"Oh, Lord, help us find Ian." The tears started again and her heart ached. It seemed strange that she loved this boy so much already, the boy she'd only known for a week. But she loved him. She loved him as if he were her own.

The reality of the hard cold floor stopped the weeping momentarily as she reached for her robe and slippers. Trudging through the dark house, she was able to avoid furniture. Every chair, every table had been in the same place for years, so she could navigate without so much as a night-light.

It was well before dawn, but Jo knew that she would not sleep again that night. Sitting on the couch, she reached out in the silence and the darkness. Scripture verses, long tucked away in memory, began to come freshly to her mind. From Isaiah . . .

Thou wilt keep him in perfect peace, whose mind is stayed on thee: because he trusteth in thee.

From Philippians . . .

Be careful for nothing; but in every thing by prayer and supplication with thanksgiving let your requests be made known unto God.

From Psalms . . .

Cast thy burden upon the Lord, and he shall sustain thee: he shall never suffer the righteous to be moved.

She recited them in her mind again. And again.

Another from Psalms came to mind . . .

"For he shall give his angels charge over thee, to keep thee in all thy ways."

Jo said it aloud. Then reciting again part of the Philippians passage:

"And the peace of God, which passeth all understanding, shall keep your hearts and minds through Christ Jesus."

Jo prayed aloud. "Oh, God. Guard Ian." Suddenly she had a mental picture of angels hovering around Ian.

"Surround my heart with peace," she said softly. With that, the darkness faded and it was morning. She was still sitting upright on the couch when she opened her eyes.

Ian thought that the world was surely coming to an end! The sudden blaring not only rattled his eardrums but also rumbled deep inside his chest. He must get away from this monster! he thought. Crawling to the door of his room, he didn't really care if someone found him on the other side. He just knew that he had to get away from the noise. Quickly he opened the door, crawled out, and shut it behind him. He could still hear the sound, but at least it wasn't as loud as before. Sweat was already running down his face, and his head pounded.

He sat in the darkened hallway and tried to make himself think. *What awful thing could have made such a racket?* he wondered. And then he realized that the rude sound was actually music, and it was coming primarily from inside his room.

He waited to see if it would stop. After a long time, it did stop, but Ian was afraid to go back inside his room. He listened. There were voices coming from down below his perch. He couldn't hear the words clearly. In fact, he couldn't hear anything clearly. He was afraid his hearing was gone for good.

With his hands over his ears he rhymed,
Hear. Hear/Hear with your ears.

Jo didn't feel like getting dressed up in her usual suit and hat, but she forced herself to put on a nice dress, something appropriate for Sunday worship. Clutching her Bible, she walked the two blocks to the church.

"Morning, Miz Anderson," a deacon who was a greeter said to her sympathetically.

"Morning," she returned the greeting. She turned the corner hoping to avoid many more sad and pathetic looks, but more than that, she hoped to avoid questions about Ian's whereabouts or the search for him.

Irene, Clara, Jean, and Eloise came out of nowhere, it seemed, and surrounded Jo with hugs and concern.

"We've been up since before dawn praying for you and Ian," said Clara.

Jo really didn't feel like hearing their fawning words, but she tried to be polite. "Me too. Thanks," she replied and hurried into the sanctuary, taking her usual seat on the third row center.

The organist began the prelude with a huge chord that Bach himself would have been proud of. The stark sound hushed the chattering crowd suddenly. Some tried to speak above the music. But most got quiet and prepared for worship. The choir began to emerge from two doors under the baptistery, filing into four neat rows.

Brother Brewton walked into the sanctuary from the back, stopping to shake a few hands and to say a word of welcome to visitors and those who had returned from vacations or extended illnesses. As if planned, he ascended the pulpit just as the organist played the final chord.

"Good morning," he said heartily.

"Good morning," the congregation replied robotically.

"I know this is a little out of the ordinary, since we usually begin our services with the call to worship, but I would like for us to all bow our heads at this moment and pray specifically for a need in our church," the pastor said.

Jo remembered that Miss Gussie Ward, a charter member of the church, had been ill for some time and was at death's door. Jo bowed her head and began to pray for Miss Gussie.

"As you all know, there is a little boy missing from our midst." Jo looked up, surprised.

The pastor continued, "We need to pray for this young man. His name is Ian Lane. We need to pray for his safety, for his safe return, and for peace for his sweet great-aunt Jo."

Jo blushed at the sound of her own name, but she knew that the pastor was sincere in his concern and was sensitive to her grief.

"Let us pray," he began.

Jo's eyes filled with tears about the same time that her heart began to fill with peace. A hand touched her shoulder, then another and another. As the pastor prayed, she felt the presence of her sisters and brothers around her whispering their own prayers to God. But the touch of them was no more real than the touch she felt from heaven. It was as though she were being lifted up, suspended on petitions to the throne room of God.

Ian opened the door slightly, vowing to close it quickly should the blaring music begin again. He listened. He recognized the voice. The man from the kitchen was standing behind the large speaker's desk and was apparently addressing someone. Ian cracked the door open a little wider and then some more. Slowly he crawled in again and looked through the mesh screen, noticing that there were people sitting on the benches listening to the man talk. This was the first time he'd actually seen the man. Of course, he was seeing only the top of his head, but from this vantage point, the man looked rather young. He spoke with the same kind inflection he had had with the cats. This man was in charge at this church. *Maybe he's the pastor,* Ian thought.

He suddenly remembered the pastor at his parents' funeral. Then he remembered Aunt Jo again. He wondered if she cared where he was. He wondered if she was looking for him. He missed her a little bit, but he decided not to dwell on it. Instead, he listened to the pastor's words.

"Now the word of the Lord came unto Jonah the son of Amittai, saying, Arise, go to Nineveh, that great city, and cry against it; for their wickedness is come up before me. But Jonah rose up to flee unto Tarshish from the presence of the Lord."

Ian had never heard such words. Amittai, Nineveh, Tarshish. Were they places near here? Ian suddenly remembered that he didn't even know where "here" was.

"But the Lord sent out a great wind into the sea, and there was a mighty tempest in the sea, so that the ship was like to be broken. Then the mariners were afraid, and cried every man unto his god, and cast forth the wares that were in the ship into the sea, to lighten it of them. But Jonah was gone down into the sides of the ship; and he lay, and was fast asleep."

Ian lay down on his stomach, propped his elbows on the floor, cupped his chin in his hands, and listened to the story. He could remember his mother telling him stories. They were about Hansel and Gretel and Jack and the Beanstalk. But that was a long time ago. He didn't remember ever hearing this story.

"So the shipmaster came to him, and said unto him, What meanest thou, O sleeper? arise, call upon thy God, if so be that God will think upon us, that we perish not. . . .

"So they took up Jonah, and cast him forth into the sea: and the sea ceased from her raging. Then the men feared the Lord exceedingly, and offered a sacrifice unto the Lord, and made vows. Now the Lord had prepared a great fish to swallow up Jonah. And Jonah was in the belly of the fish three days and three nights."

Ian almost laughed out loud. Once he'd seen on TV where a shark ate a man's leg, but he'd never heard about a fish swallowing a man who lived to tell about it. But the pastor kept telling the story as if he really believed it, and the people sitting on the benches didn't seem the least bit skeptical either. Ian figured there might be something to the story, so he kept on listening.

Refused. That was the first "R" in the pastor's speech. Apparently the man, Jonah, hadn't wanted to go to the town his God had told him to visit. It wasn't really clear to Ian why Jonah refused, but that was not what caught Ian's attention. It was the second "R."

Jonah "ran," and that was something Ian understood perfectly. Even then, Ian marveled at his own spontaneous bolt from Aunt Jo's. He didn't even remember thinking, plotting, planning. He had just run. Of course, he had found refuge, but still he was running.

The next part of the speech was funny. The pastor

talked about what could have been inside that big fish. The pastor called a boy younger than Ian to the stage and asked him if he liked to fish. The boy nodded. The pastor asked the boy what he used for bait. The boy shyly said "Worms!" The whole crowd roared. It wasn't such a funny answer. It was that the little boy said it in a loud, slow drawl.

The pastor asked the audience other things that could have been inside that big fish. A teenager said, "Seaweed." A man said, "Other dead fish." The people laughed again.

"Worms, seaweed, dead fish," the pastor said with a smile in his voice and looked at his audience. "Can you imagine the smell?" The idea, Ian surmised, is that running away could end a person in an awful, smelly place. But Ian looked at his own surroundings. Except for the lumpy mattress he slept on, he was certainly no worse for the wear. He lay back on the mattress and tried to tune out the rest of the speech. He did, however, want to listen enough to hear if there was another "R" word. There was. Repented. This was a word that Ian had never heard, but he figured it meant that Jonah had returned home. That was something that Ian was not willing to do, at least not then. It was too risky, but Ian couldn't even figure out why.

Suddenly Ian was afraid. *Run, run/It's no fun/Run, run/ It's no fun.* He closed his eyes and tried to focus on the pastor's speech. He couldn't. Then finally the pastor stopped the speech and asked everyone to pray with him. The man spoke out loud, a prayer like poetry almost but without rhyme. The rhythmic lilt, however, caught Ian's ear, and when the pastor's voice became impassioned, Ian was slightly embarrassed to be eavesdropping on this intimate conversation this pastor was obviously having with his God. The final words of the prayer were like the lyrics to a song, "We ask these things in Your Son's name. Amen."

The sweet lull was suddenly broken with the sound of the monster beating on his chest once again. *Oh, the music,* Ian thought, as he slapped his hands over his ears. His body shook from the electricity still pulsating through the raw nerves of his eardrums. But before he crawled out the big door to safety, Ian glanced down and discovered the source of the commotion. A woman with gray matted hair and painted fingernails was pounding the black and white keys of a keyboard. Her feet seemed to be moving about, causing the music as well, and Ian made a mental note. This woman was making loud music, and therefore he would need to watch her carefully from then on. Whenever her hands and feet started to move, he should run for the hills.

When the music stopped, Ian moved back into his home. Looking out over the people milling around, Ian saw kind wrinkled faces smiling and greeting the others. The pastor was getting hugs from several women and hearty backslaps from elderly gentlemen wearing dark suits and ties. Some of them leaned into the young preacher as if they did not want to miss a single word of his blessing to them. One man slyly slipped something into the pastor's coat pocket, and still another presented what looked like folded money in the grip of his friendly handshake.

There were a few children, Ian noticed, other than the little one who gave the worm answer. Ian saw a couple of toddlers, a girl about Ian's age, and a tall preteenaged boy. The others, though, were older than Aunt Jo was. Aunt Jo. He dismissed the memory, curled up on his mattress, and waited for silence to surround him again.

Chapter Eight

By Monday morning,

the Crestview Police Department had received several reports of sightings of ten-year-old boys who matched Ian's description. One turned out to be a little boy named Josh who did look somewhat like Ian Lane but who checked out to be exactly who he had claimed to be. The others were seriously investigated but did not lead the officers to Ian. A young boy, however, was caught playing hooky from school and promptly brought to his parents' attention with a serious warning and a promise to send the boy to the juvenile judge the next time he was caught leaving school grounds without authorization.

Jo was frustrated and exhausted. She tried to eat some of the comfort food in the refrigerator, but it only made her stomach queasier.

Frank Benson's shoulders slumped as he walked into his office building. He sighed heavily. Marilyn, his secretary, greeted him and then handed him a mug of fresh coffee with one hand and a thin stack of pink message slips and that day's mail with the other. Frank mumbled a "good morning" without really looking up. He pushed the door to his inner office open with his foot and laid the coffee cup and mail stack on his already paper-strewn desk. Shuffling through the "please call" messages, Frank stopped on the one that read, "Please call Walter Patton at the police department." And on the lines below it, it read, "Regarding: fire marshal report in."

"That's fast," Frank said out loud.

It was early, Ian knew, but how early in the morning, he was not sure. He wondered if anybody came to the church on, what was it, Monday morning. He listened for sounds of people for maybe five minutes before he moved. The crackers and juice had filled his hunger the day before, but he wondered if he should be bold and return to the kitchen to see if he could find variety to his diet.

The auditorium lights were off, but sunlight came through a window that looked like it was filled with broken glass. It projected a kaleidoscope of color on the burgundy carpet near the speaker's stand. Ian looked up at the window above the back row of seats. At first it looked like the torn pieces of colored cellophane he had used in an art project at the new school in Crestview. He had arranged them in a random pattern on a piece of poster board. His teacher had

70

said that it was a beautiful collage and then asked him what it represented. Ian had had no idea how to answer, so he had just shrugged his shoulders. But when he had looked at the pattern again, he had seen an abstract image that had resembled a flame. Quickly he had torn the poster board in shreds. He had wadded the torn pieces together and had thrown them in the trash can at the back of the class. He had told his teacher that he had made a mistake and needed to start over.

Ian looked up again at the window. He did not recognize any picture. They were just disjointed shards of glass.

Abbie woke up with a mild headache. She lay in bed for a few minutes and listened to the rattling in the kitchen. She knew that Jim was trying to make breakfast for her. The rattling stopped for a moment, and Jim appeared at the bedroom door.

"Oh, hi," Jim said sweetly, sitting by her on the bed. "Hope I didn't wake you up. I was looking for that little pancake-maker thing you use to make, you know, pancakes."

Abbie smiled. "The griddle, you mean?"

"Yeah. I can't find it. I know how you love pancakes, and I wanted to make you some."

Abbie used to make pancakes for them when they were in seminary. But she really didn't like pancakes as much as Jim did.

She groaned.

"What's the matter? Are you feeling bad?" Jim asked.

"Just a little headachy, that's all." Abbie tried to sit up in bed, but even that made her dizzy and nauseous. She lay back down flat.

"I'm calling the doctor," Jim said, dashing out the bedroom door before she could protest.

Throwing back the covers on the bed, Abbie saw that her legs and ankles were more swollen than ever. They had swelled sometimes while she was upright but never like this after reclining for a whole night. At her last visit two weeks before, the doctor had said that some swelling was normal. He had checked her blood pressure and had said it was high normal. He had said to get plenty of rest, lay off salt, and elevate her legs. She had done what the doctor ordered.

She could hear Jim talking on the phone in the other room. His voice was high-pitched and stressed. He sounded frightened. Abbie tried to listen, but she was distracted by the headache that was getting worse.

Jim reappeared, but this time he looked blurry, like she was looking at him through the shower door.

"Abbie, the doctor said you should come in right now." Jim looked at her swollen legs and feet and let out a gasp.

"Jim . . ." And suddenly she couldn't speak. It was as if her tongue were paralyzed.

Mercy and Hope were meowing somewhere in the building. Ian figured that the pastor had arrived and was getting their food bowls ready in the kitchen. After several minutes, however, when the cats hadn't stopped calling for their breakfast, he wondered what was taking so long.

Ian's stomach was growling too, and obviously he had missed his window of opportunity to slip down to the kitchen and find his own meal. He poured himself a small cup of grape juice and ate three crackers, this time with peanut butter, to fill the hunger for a while.

Minutes passed and the meowing got louder. Apparently the cats were searching other ways to satisfy their morning hungries too.

Ian looked down into the auditorium to see if anyone was around. One of the doors to the outer room was open, he could tell, and suddenly he saw the cats run down the aisle meowing heartily. While one seemed to be on a mission to find food, the other seemed to be more interested in playtime. The tabby pounced on the calico from behind, and a wrestling match began. Ian didn't know which cat was which, so he figured he'd call the tabby Mercy and the calico Hope. They didn't seem to mind what they were called as long as someone fed them.

Mercy was bigger and was dominating the match. They tumbled several times in a ball of mixed fur and tails, and finally Mercy had Hope by the back of the neck. Using her hind legs, Mercy thumped her opponent playfully until Hope could escape the grasp. Upright, Hope squared off like a pro wrestler and, with ears back, hissed at the other. Both cats then ran out the door and disappeared from Ian's sight.

"Oh, well, I guess they're grumpy when they get hungry," Ian said aloud. Suddenly Ian recognized his own voice and put his hand over his mouth.

Quiet, quiet, not a sound/Or you'll finally be found.

The rhyme reminded Ian of his runaway status. He vowed to be more careful and to lie low at all times.

The sun was behind him as he turned onto the interstate. Frank had told Marilyn to cancel all of his appointments for the day. He was going to be in Crestview again to try to find the boy.

As he drove, Frank Benson wasn't sure what he was going to say to the great-aunt. He had good news, but he was sure that Josephine Anderson would hardly think so if she still hadn't found Ian Lane.

The morning news showed the picture of Ian again. Even though this was the same picture they had shown many times before, Jo thought that the little boy looked tired and hungry. *No,* she thought, *maybe it's me who's tired and hungry.*

Pouring herself a glass of cold milk, Jo sat down at the kitchen table and tried to pray. She couldn't quite get the words out. The pain was deep and the exhaustion was debilitating. All she could do was cry.

Jim couldn't think straight. There was so much going on around him and inside him, he couldn't even conjure up a memory. He tried to go back over the past few days with Abbie, to try to figure out what signals he hadn't picked up on, what he could have done to have prevented this.

Just then a toddler cried out through a croupy cough. An old man leaned forward from his chair and tried to stand up. A younger woman, maybe the man's daughter, yelled at him to sit down. Some of the nurses were chattering to one another while one was talking to someone on the phone. The TV was tuned to a local morning news show, and the face of a small boy appeared on the screen.

Jim sat in disbelief. Just an hour before he had seen his wife's body start to convulse. Panicked, he had called 9-1-1, and within minutes the paramedics were wheeling Abbie out the door and into an ambulance. *How could this have happened?* he wondered. *What went wrong?*

A nurse turned up the volume on the TV to hear the news bulletin over the hubbub of the waiting room. Jim was annoyed. He was already confused and couldn't think what he should be doing right then. Maybe he should call somebody. Who?

A man in hospital scrubs tapped Jim on the shoulder. Jim jumped nervously.

"Reverend Copeland?" the man asked.

Jim sprang to his feet, making him eye-to-eye with the emergency room physician.

The boredom and the hunger were getting rather unbearable. Ian kept his eye on the open auditorium door. The cats did not return. The pastor did not appear. The only sounds were those on the street outside. He guessed it was still morning, but he also guessed it had been at least an hour since he'd seen the cat spectacle.

Opening the door to his room, Ian did not see any lights on anywhere. He heard no one in the hallway either. Down the hall a little way, Ian noticed another door, one he hadn't seen before. *Probably just a closet or something,* he thought, but it was worth exploring. He turned the knob and pushed the door. It opened into another short hallway that seemed to disappear down some steps just a few feet away. Ian knew he shouldn't be too bold, but the new find looked safe and interesting. He wondered if this could be a secret passageway, a shortcut down to the kitchen.

He walked a little way and listened and then walked a

little more until he got to the top of the steps. Looking down, he saw what looked like, yeah . . .

A swimming pool, Ian said to himself. It was empty and not nearly as large as the city pool in Madison, and yet it was three times larger than his bathtub at home. Slowly, Ian crept down the stairs and found the water faucet. As quietly as possible, he turned the knob. Water! Sure enough, it was running water! He had heard of these things in rich people's homes. *They call them Jacuzzis,* he thought. Later, much later, in the wee hours of the night, he would let the water run awhile and fill up his spa for bathing, swimming, or just relaxing.

Jo's eyes lit up when she heard the doorbell. She was sure that it was the police bringing hungry, tired Ian home from a weekend runaway adventure. She wouldn't scold him. She wouldn't even be angry at all. She would just hold him tightly and ask him what he wanted to eat. Oh, but what if it was the police telling her that . . . no, she wouldn't believe that.

Looking out the front window, Jo didn't see a police cruiser at all, but she did recognize the car. It belonged to Frank Benson.

"Good morning, Miz Anderson," Frank said as Jo opened the door. He couldn't believe how exhausted she looked. He knew, then, that the boy had not been found. He almost hated to show her the fire marshal's report. He knew it wouldn't matter to her that the cause of the fire had been determined as accidental. Faulty wiring. That would be good news to most insurance beneficiaries, but somehow he figured she could not care less about the large sum of money that was about to be hers.

Abbie had an IV tube taped to her hand, so Jim curled his hand around hers gently. She opened her eyes only slightly but did not regard her husband at all. She closed her eyes again.

Jim studied Abbie's fingernails. They were so delicate. Cleanly groomed but not painted. Abbie never liked to fuss over her looks. She rarely wore makeup, just a little mascara and blush on Sundays. But she didn't really need makeup. Her deep brown eyes were framed with thick black eyelashes, and her skin was flawless. Only recently had her cheeks looked flushed. Jim had even thought that she was wearing too much blush at first, but she had said she wasn't wearing any makeup at all. He didn't pick up on that as a sign of complications.

Abbie's breathing was steady and deep. Jim was glad that she could rest. The doctor had said that she had had eclampsia, a serious condition that can endanger both the mother and the baby. The only way to save the mother was to deliver the baby. The doctors had done an emergency caesarian just in time, but the baby was so small and his condition was very fragile, the doctor warned. Abbie's blood pressure was still high, but the doctor had said she would recover in time.

Jim stroked Abbie's hair. Jet-black silk is what he had thought of when he first met her. She had been in his biology class, a course that his major had required but one he had dreaded. Science had never been his thing. But when he walked into the lecture classroom on the first day, the scowl he had worn to the class melted away.

He had taken the desk directly behind hers. At first, he hadn't noticed her, but his spiral notebook slid off his desk as he sat down. Abbie had picked it up and handed it to him with the smile that made his stomach twitch. He had never believed in love at first sight, but his first glimpse of Abigail Smith, student number 112890, Biology 103, was at least a lesson in academic discipline. During each lecture, he had to force himself to listen and not daydream about the brown-eyed beauty in front of him. He looked forward to the weekly lab in which he could actually look at her straight on from across the lab table. If he hadn't caught her eye once and seen her smile at him, he would have never had the courage to talk to her, much less ask her on a date. He had soon become quite the science buff.

Jim looked up and saw a young nurse standing at the door.

"Reverend, I'm afraid I need to ask you to leave now. I'm sorry," she said.

Jim was grateful that the hospital staff had let him back to see Abbie at all. He knew many of the nurses there because he visited church members on a regular basis. They let the pastor bend the rules.

"When will the doctor be back in?" Jim asked.

"He's on the floor now, and I told him you wanted to see him again," the nurse said softly, leading Jim out the unit door. Finally, he had thought of the questions he wanted to ask the doctor. He had been in shock before and could hardly even remember his own name. He wasn't even sure exactly what he had put on the admission forms when they brought Abbie in.

"The neonatal unit is one floor up, Reverend. Would you like to go up and check on your son?"

Ian stripped all of his clothes off and slipped into the warm water. He had never really liked to take a bath, but this was different. There was no soap or washcloth on the edge of the tub. This was a luxury.

A heavy burgundy curtain closed off the Jacuzzi from the auditorium. He had closed the entrance door behind him, so he knew this was a private swim. The basin wasn't big enough to do elaborate swimming strokes. And besides, he didn't want to make splashing noises just in case somebody happened to come into the room. So he floated on his back, letting the warm water bathe him, soothe him, and take him back to a rare happy memory.

"I'm a fish," Ian had squealed, floating faceup in the tub as his mother stood over him smiling.

"Oh, you are. What kind of fish are you?" she had asked.

"I'm a Ian fish," he had said. And his mother had laughed out loud.

That was the last time he remembered her laughing. That's not to say she didn't laugh after that; he just didn't remember, that's all.

Floating on the water, Ian savored the memory, drifting away, trying to recite his favorite poem. Finally he remembered how it started. *Dark brown is the river, golden is the sand. . . .*

"I just want to fluff and twirl these silks," a voice spoke suddenly.

Ian's reaction to the sound could have given him away. His first response was to frantically start trying to get to his clothes on the edge of the tub. Then he remembered that there was a large curtain covering the opening to his private spa. Before he made much of a noise, he stopped, wrapped his arms around his naked body, and listened.

"Mattie Ruth, you fuss over those plants like they were real," said another voice.

"I don't understand it. I come in here once a week and fix these ferns, and lo and behold if by Sunday morning they aren't all mashed and lopsided."

"Reckon George moves 'em around while he's vacuuming the carpet?"

"You can't do this much mashing by just vacuuming, Sue Ellen. He must run over 'em with a bulldozer to get 'em this flat on one side."

Ian figured these two were some of the older ladies he had seen yesterday. They talked as they rearranged the plants.

"Well, you know George has that drinking problem."

"No!"

"Oh, yeah, why do you think his face is so red all the time?"

"I thought it was because he worked outside so much."

"Oh, heavens, no. He's as good at elbow bendin' as anybody I've ever seen."

"I'm shocked. Why, we can't have somebody on our staff that drinks. I'll have to bring this up at the next church council meeting."

"Oh, don't tell them who told you, Sue Ellen. Far be it from me to gossip . . ."

"How long has it been since I put that bread in?"

Bread?

"'Bout twenty minutes, I think."

"I need to check on it and start the fruit salad."

Fruit salad. The voices trailed off just as Ian's mouth began to water. He figured that these ladies were cooking down in the kitchen for some occasion. He hoped that the occasion was an early luncheon and that they would vacate the building after that so he could explore the leftovers.

"Apparently, Miz Anderson, Ian's parents had kept a life insurance policy on themselves. The beneficiary, of course, is Ian," Frank Benson told Jo. Jo winced. Just the mention of Ian's name made her heart ache.

"That should be put into a fund for his college," Jo said.

"Of course, some of the money will go to pay the funeral expenses. What is left over is, well . . . let's just say it's a sizable sum. The company will cut a check this week."

"Suppose that'll send him to college, if he invests it now," Jo said.

"Miz Anderson, that'll not only send him to college but will buy his only living relative a lot of nice things." Jo didn't like anything about this man, especially the way he talked about money.

"Thank you, Mr. Benson," she said and tried to close the door.

"Oh, and the Lanes also had homeowner's coverage with our company. Since the fire was determined an accident, there will be an extra $200,000 paid for the loss of the house and its contents, but if Ian is not found, you being his legal guardian . . ."

Jo stepped forward and stomped her foot.

"Ian will be found, Mr. Benson, and he will go to college, and get a job, and have a family, and use his money any way he chooses. I'm going to see to it that he does!" Jo stormed off into the bedroom, leaving Frank Benson to see himself off the front porch.

His father loved him at first sight, but James Bradford Copeland didn't even look like a human being. At just over two pounds, he looked more like a hairless puppy. The tubes that ran in and out of the small body made Jim realize just how sick his newborn son was.

Jim leaned against the plate-glass window, weary and numb. *This should be a time of celebration,* he thought, but instead he was in mourning. He prayed, *Oh, God, breathe Your strength into my son's little body. And, Lord, draw out the poison in Abbie's.*

A young woman in a bathrobe and slippers shuffled up to the window next to him.

"Which one is yours?" she asked.

"That one." Jim pointed.

"How much did he weigh?" the woman asked.

"Two pounds, four ounces," Jim said, marveling that he could recall his own son's birth weight after the flurry of activity and stress.

"Small. Mine weighed three and a half. She's breathing on her own," the woman said proudly.

Jim couldn't breathe himself all of a sudden. The lump in his throat finally erupted into sobs. The mother looked at him with empathy.

"This is a good neonatal unit. I'm sure your son will be fine." The woman touched his convulsing shoulder. Jim had stood by many grieving families, widows, and widowers, to give a touch of compassion and words of comfort. He had buried other people's children and old saints of God, but he had never himself felt this kind of grief and despair. It was then that he realized that he hadn't called anyone with the news. Not even his family. He had been instructed to call Abbie's parents the minute she went into labor. He had promised to call his mother too and several church members who had vowed their prayers and support. Jim didn't even have his address book with all the phone numbers in it.

After a good cry—the third one that morning—Jo picked up the phone.

"Okaloosa County Sheriff's Department," the receptionist answered.

"I need to talk to the sheriff, please. This is Josephine Anderson." Jo tried not to sound too upset.

"Hey, Miz Anderson," the sheriff said as he came on the line, sounding sympathetic and a little apologetic.

There was one thing that Jo Anderson would not tolerate, and that was pity. She cleared her throat, wiped her nose with a tissue, and spoke with determination.

"So, any information on my boy?" she asked.

"No, ma'am. Not a word. We've done everything we can think of to help find that boy." He tried to sound encouraging.

"Wel, then, that's not enough. He's been gone for three days now, and every minute we wait, the harder it will be to find him," Jo argued.

"Yes, ma'am, I know, but we don't know what else to do," the sheriff said calmly.

"Maybe you need to broaden your search," Jo said.

"Ma'am?"

"Well, maybe you need to look outside the state line. Maybe he got all the way over in Alabama or Georgia."

"Now, Miz Anderson, let us handle this investigation. We know what we're doing," the sheriff tried to explain.

"Well, apparently not. There's no telling how far he

could have gotten in three days."

"But a boy that age . . . ," the sheriff tried to interrupt.

"Now Ian Lane is out who-knows-where thinking who-knows-what, and if you won't look for him, I'll have to take matters into my own hands," Jo said forcefully and hung up the phone. She resolved not to cry anymore but to take action. She remembered the leftovers in her refrigerator. Though she wasn't hungry, she knew she'd need her strength to do what she knew she had to do.

The leftovers were scrumptious. Ian couldn't remember when he'd had such a meal. It looked like there was a dish containing every food group. Meat, vegetables, fruit, grains. The plastic containers were stacked neatly in the refrigerator as if the ladies were preparing for an inspection. Ian was careful, though, to make sure that the three bites or so he took from each one could never be detected. He meticulously tamped down each scoop of salad or casserole or butter beans. He rearranged the rolls left on the plate so that they still formed a perfectly round circle. All the foods were cold, but Ian knew that this was a sacrifice he'd have to make to survive.

The building was so quiet. He didn't even hear Mercy and Hope anywhere. He wondered if they were curled up in a corner somewhere taking afternoon naps. He thought that a nap might be a good idea for him, so he climbed the stairs to the auditorium and was going to go back to his perch when he heard a door open and close behind him in the kitchen. He shot up the stairs quickly but quietly and hid behind the benches, listening to see who had entered.

This seemed to be a happy intruder. He or she was

whistling a lilting tune, although Ian didn't recognize it. He had never heard the pastor whistle—hum, yes, but not whistle. He wondered who else might have access to the kitchen door. Ian began to sweat when he thought about how close he had come to getting caught in the kitchen.

Chapter Nine

It was midafternoon

before Jo could get on the road. She had to tell her neighbors where she was going, cash a check at the bank, put gas in the car, and pack a few clothes. She didn't dare tell Jean or her other friends for fear they would talk her out of it.

"Internet this, database that," Jo huffed as she pulled out of the driveway. "The only way to find my boy is with a little talk and a lot of shoe leather."

By the time she got to the Madison exit, there were only a few rooms left at the Days Inn. She forced herself to eat a light dinner at the local diner.

"You haven't seen this little boy, have you?" Jo asked the waitress, showing her the posters she had had made with a current picture of Ian on them.

"Oh, that's the little feller on the news, ain't he?" the waitress asked.

"Yes, his name is Ian Lane. He used to live here, but his

parents were killed in a fire." Jo started giving as much information as she thought she needed to get the woman to recognize Ian.

"Lady, I'm not from around here, but Lillian, she owns the place and is a native, and she'll know what you're talking about." The waitress poured Jo more sweet tea and quickly went to the back.

Jo admitted to herself that she had no idea what she was doing, but she had to do something. Sitting at home and crying was not helping Ian at all.

"Oh, yeah. You're the boy's aunt, aren't you?" asked an older woman, who Jo figured was the Lillian who owned the place.

"Yes, I am. I'm Josephine Anderson. Ian is my great-nephew," Jo said, a little more hopeful.

"I'll bet you're about worried to death over that little boy." Lillian seemed to be sweet and genuinely concerned.

"I am, but the police can't seem to do anything, and I figured I'd hunt for him myself," Jo said.

"I don't blame you a bit. Where else have you looked?"

"Nowhere, really. I thought I'd start here and work my way back west. I couldn't sit there in Crestview a minute longer. I don't know; I just thought he might have come back here since this was the only home he'd ever known," Jo said, taking a bite of corn bread.

"Well, I haven't seen the boy since, I don't know, since before his tragedy. I saw him every now and then walking by here, I guessed on his way to the store. He'd go this way, and after awhile he'd go the other with two or three grocery sacks full," Lillian remembered. "Word has it that his parents were drunks and that he had to take . . ." Lillian caught herself.

"It's OK. I know that Mary and Ed were alcoholics. I

didn't really have much contact with them. In fact, I hardly knew little Ian myself," Jo tried to explain.

"Well, honey, I just hope you find him," Lillian said sympathetically.

"Would you be willing to put one of Ian's posters up in your window?" Jo asked.

"Sure, honey." And Lillian disappeared to the back of the restaurant.

It didn't take long for the word to spread about Abbie and the baby. Before an hour had passed, the church and the pastorium filled up with food and prayer warriors. Many of the men of the church sat in a room at the hospital and waited for their pastor to emerge. They were prepared to keep an all-night vigil if they needed to.

"No change," Jim said as he greeted a room full of his own parishioners. He was surprised to see so many of his church members eagerly awaiting the news of the condition of his wife and child. The young pastor looked ten years older than he was. The dark circles under his eyes and the day-old beard made the usually clean-cut man look more like some of the people he'd visit on Saturdays in the inner-city housing projects. His eyes welled with tears as each person touched him with a hug or word of comfort.

When Ian woke up, it was night already. At least it was dark. He listened for sound. He heard nothing. He figured that it might be safe to venture back into the kitchen for another round of leftovers. In fact, he decided to launch his refrigerator raids at night when he was surer the coast would be clear. He didn't want to take the chance again of being found.

Chapter Ten

Jo was surprised

that she'd slept so well. She reasoned she had been so exhausted that her body collapsed in spite of the fact she was in a motel bed and burdened for Ian. Before she got out of bed, Jo voiced a prayer thanking God for letting her sleep.

The school yard was already full of children by the time Jo got there. She was relieved to find that the schools were still in session. She thought that it might be harder to talk to Ian's former teachers if they had already started their summer vacations.

"Yes, Missus Anderson, we knew Ian very well here. We were so saddened about his parents' death, and we're truly concerned about his disappearance." The school principal was articulate and quite sincere.

"I don't know where else to turn," Jo began. "The police have not been able to find a trace of him. I thought I'd look around for him myself. I don't know why I came here, but I thought I'd just see if I could learn about Ian and think like him, so I could figure out where he'd go."

"Well, anything we can do, Missus Anderson, we'll gladly do."

"For starters, you can put up some of these posters on your bulletin boards. I saw one in the hall as I came in." Jo counted out five posters and laid them on the principal's desk.

"But all the children know Ian and what he looks like."

Jo sighed.

The principal continued, "We'll put up the posters, Missus Anderson. Would you like to talk to the last teacher Ian had?" the principal turned to look at her class schedule.

Jo smiled. *It's a start,* she thought.

Ian was awakened by the sound. It was soft and slightly muffled, but he recognized it as the pastor's voice. He seemed to be talking to someone, but Ian did not detect another voice talking back. Quietly Ian peered through his mesh wall into the auditorium. As soon as his eyes adapted to the light, Ian could see the pastor lying facedown in front of the big table where the Bible lay. Ian couldn't understand the pastor's words because he seemed to be talking and crying at the same time.

The pastor lay perfectly still for almost a minute. Ian was wondering if the man had gone to sleep. But within a few seconds, the pastor rose slowly and sat upright resting his elbows on his knees. Ian figured he could hear the man's voice better this way.

"Oh, God. Oh, God," the pastor kept repeating. Ian realized that the pastor must have been engaged in prayer.

Frank had the Ian Lane case on his mind at all times. The insurance agent had communicated with the company he represented, and he had informed the client's beneficiary of the coming payments. He had done everything by the book, he thought, but there was more to this case than that. Frank stirred at his eggs and didn't even notice Lillian standing over his shoulder.

"Penny for your thoughts, Frank," Lillian said, pouring him a second cup of coffee.

"Thanks, Lillian. I don't know where I was," Frank tried to explain.

"It's that boy, isn't it?"

"Yeah, I've done all I was supposed to do, but somehow . . ."

"Well, that boy's aunt isn't giving up, I'll tell you."

"How do you know that?" Frank asked.

"She was here at suppertime yesterday and was asking about him," Lillian said.

"Here? In Madison? Jo is here?"

"Yeah, she gave me a poster to put up of the boy. Didn't you see it in the window?"

"I guess I didn't," Frank said.

"She was asking a lot of questions about him. I got the feeling she was gonna look for him herself. Think she's staying out at the Days Inn."

Frank took a final sip of the coffee, laid some cash on the table, and left the diner with an absentminded "thanks" to Lillian.

✦ ✦ ✦

Ian propped his head on his hands as if he were listening to another of the pastor's stories. It was an interesting thing to watch, for sure, but there was no plotline. The man kept talking as if he were asking a question and then waiting quietly for a response. He would ask, "Where can I go?" Again he would ask such questions and then pause as if listening for a response. Ian looked to make sure the man wasn't talking on a cell phone or something. He wasn't, but the man was obviously involved in a two-way conversation.

Suddenly a phone rang. It sounded like a cell phone. Ian thought it was ironic that the phone rang at that moment, just as he was thinking about that.

The pastor reached in his back pocket and pulled out the ringing phone.

"Hello?"

Ian's curiosity was piqued.

"Yes," the pastor said to the caller. "I'll be right there." And the man made a quick exit out the front door of the building.

+ + +

Jo had to wait until Mrs. Barkley had a break from her class. Finally, the pleasant-looking woman walked into the teachers' lounge and sat down beside Jo on the leather couch.

"What can I do for you, Missus Anderson?" the young teacher asked.

"I'm looking for Ian, and I just wanted to see if I could figure out where he might have run off to." Jo felt an immediate bond with the teacher.

"Are you pretty sure he's hiding and not, well . . . you know?" the teacher had to ask.

"The police are treating this like a runaway case, not an

abduction. I think they're right about that at least. Mrs. Barkley, I've just got to believe he's run off somewhere and not met with any harm. I've got to believe it. He's probably hiding somewhere scared to death," Jo said, letting the tears come to her eyes for the first time that day.

"I understand, and I'll tell you everything I know about him from the year I had him in my class," said Mrs. Barkley. "I just hope it'll help."

"Thank you so much," Jo responded, touching the teacher's soft hand.

Most of it was not new information. Jo knew, of course, of the habits of her niece. Apparently the Lanes had both had drinking problems since Ed's accident right after Ian was born. Jo had known that Ed's injuries were crippling, not to the extent that he could not walk, but that the many surgeries that he had had could not relieve the pain. Instead of resorting to more therapy or medication, Ed had numbed the pain with alcohol. Mary had tried to encourage Ed to file a lawsuit against the other driver, but for some reason Ed preferred to drown the sorrows in bourbon. Finally, when Ed's disability approval came, Mary was already starting to join Ed in his addiction. Mary had refused any help offered by her aunt Josephine, but she never returned the cash Aunt Jo sent to Ian.

According to Mrs. Barkley, social services had been called many times to the Lane house. Each time an investigator would look at the living conditions and the treatment of the child and find nothing that would constitute removing Ian from his parents' home. There seemed to be just enough care taken by the parents to have social services leave them alone, at least for another year, until another of Ian's teachers became concerned about him.

The more Jo talked to Ian's teacher, the more she realized that the roles had become reversed in his house. Ian had not only become self-sufficient, but also had become his parents' caretaker.

Ian was glad he had decided to stay in his room and eat grape juice and crackers for his midday meal. The whistling started as a faint sound down in the basement kitchen. Ian was fairly sure this was not the pastor. The whistler was somebody else, maybe an employee of the church. Maybe it was George that the two ladies had talked about. He would call him George anyway.

The meowing was a welcome sound. Mercy and Hope scooted into the auditorium and started their antics again as before. The footsteps up the steps made the cats stop and scramble for cover.

"There you are, you urchins!" The man speaking was old and haggard and disheveled. The cats lay low as the old man approached with a broom. He swatted at them, and they scrambled back out the auditorium door.

The old man was mumbling to himself. "Stinkin' cats. Just make my life more miserable, is all." The whistling began again as George went about cleaning the room. He vacuumed the carpet thoroughly; he dusted the table and picked up a few stray pieces of paper on the benches. Within an hour, the man had finished cleaning the room. Ian listened for at least another hour as the man apparently went about cleaning other rooms in the building. He heard chairs scraping on tile floors, the vacuum cleaner running, some more whistling, and then the hard bumping sound of what he thought was the basement door closing. Ian listened for maybe another half an hour. He didn't hear a single sound, so he figured that the man was gone for the afternoon.

Ian was full of crackers, canned tuna, and juice, and he was not sleepy at all. It was time for a swim. Floating in the warm water, Ian tried to figure out what was going on with the pastor. He had been so sad and so passionate in his conversation and then so quickly gone when the phone call came. However, Ian couldn't be too concerned about the man's problems; he had his own survival to think of. As soon as it became dark again, Ian ventured down into the kitchen. This time he would need to come back with a little stash of food to hold him for another day.

Frank had been in college when the accident happened. His mother had called him at his dorm and assured him that his father was all right and that there was no need to come home. She had said, however, that the man driving the other car had not fared as well. He had been critically injured and was not supposed to survive. Frank had been relieved to hear that his father was all right, and since he hadn't known the other guy, an Ed Lane, he didn't give it another thought. When Frank had come home for his Thanksgiving break, he had found out that the man had survived, but that he was making a very slow recovery.

In the nine years since, Frank had learned a lot about that night, and he had been as diligent as his parents had been at keeping the details from becoming public. Still, he didn't understand why the fire was necessary. He had tried to convince his father that Ed Lane would never make good on his threats to expose the "arrangement," but Charles Benson's paranoia had apparently grown with the years, and he would not wait the situation out. Now, with the fiery deaths and with the survival of little Ian, Frank knew that the case might not lie dormant anymore. He had no choice but to actively join in the cover-up.

Chapter Eleven

The knock on Jo's motel

room door came just as she was about to leave. Her bag was packed, and she figured that the knock might be housekeeping coming to remake the room for the next guest. She was surprised to see Frank Benson.

"Hello, Miz Anderson," Frank said with a forced smile.

"Well, Mr. Benson, how did you know I was here?" Jo asked with some suspicion.

"I heard yesterday that you were here looking for the boy." Frank pushed his way into the room. "I went by the school, but you'd just left there. I came by here a couple of times, but I guess we just missed each other."

"I was about to check out. I went to every place, including the cemetery, where Ian might have gone and didn't find so much as a footprint. I did find out some valuable information, though."

"Oh?"

"Yes, I found out just how grown-up Ian had become,"

Jo continued. "The lady at the grocery store said that Ian came in there every day or so with just the right amount of money to buy meals to fix for himself. She said too that he would bring in coupons from the newspaper when something was on sale. She said he'd gotten really good at pinching his pennies." The thought of that little boy fending for himself made Jo's heart break again, but she took strength in the fact that the experience had prepared him for the events of the past days. She had more hope than ever that Ian was safe somewhere. "The teller at the bank said that she had cashed a couple of his parents' checks for him too, that is, after she called them and they said it was OK."

"I see. Well, I had just heard you were in town and thought I'd see if you needed any help with anything." Frank tried to sound genuinely concerned.

"No, Mr. Benson. I'm going to start heading back home. I've got some other ideas for help in finding Ian." Jo picked up her suitcase and moved toward the door. She didn't like the feeling she got when Frank Benson was around.

Almost all of Ian's dreams had taken place around the water. He was usually floating on top of it or he was trying to rescue something else that was floating. That's why this dream was so particularly strange and frightening. The flames had gotten high in his bedroom, and he was hearing the screaming nearby. He had looked toward the window and seen it open enough for him to get out. He had climbed onto the roof and was looking down into the yard. Standing there were two men yelling for him to jump to them. He stood motionless, trying to decide to whom to jump. One man was yelling God's name as if in distress; the man had the face of the pastor. The other was yelling, "Fire! Fire!" This was the man he had seen in Aunt Jo's front room just before he ran away.

The dream ended just before Ian had jumped.

Ian poured himself a cup of grape juice and opened another pack of saltines.

Ian was glad that he looked out through the mesh before he rattled the paper on the cracker package again. There, sitting about the third row back, was a person. Ian squinted and saw that it was a lady, maybe his own mother's age, sitting completely still with her head bowed.

Just then another person entered. This was a man, older, escorting an older woman. They both took seats just across the aisle from the younger woman. They too sat quietly, holding hands, with their heads bowed.

Another man, two women, and a teenage boy walked in, sat quietly, and bowed their heads. Within minutes after that, almost all the seats were filled on the benches, with people being perfectly quiet. Then one woman began to cry softly, then another, and other women moved to these and put their arms around them.

Finally, an older man walked through the door and faced the crowd that numbered maybe a hundred by then.

"Folks, thanks so much for coming today," he said in a low, somber voice. "I've just come from the hospital. Brother Jim would be so moved to know about this impromptu prayer meeting for the baby and Abbie. I just want to report that Abbie's condition has improved somewhat. She has been moved out of ICU into a private room. She can't have visitors for a while, though, except her family. Her parents are here from Bogalusa, and, of course, Brother Jim is there." The man paused and took a shaky breath. "I'm afraid," he continued, "that the news is not as good on baby James. He died this morning." The crowd gasped, and the crying women cried even louder. The man's voice quivered. "Brother Jim was with him when he died. The sweet thing did not suffer." And then the man broke down and cried too.

Ian deduced that the pastor referred to was the man he had heard speak to the crowd and to an Unseen Person. Pastor Jim. And Abbie, he guessed, was Jim's wife. Baby James must have been the pastor's son. Ian's heart was sad too, even though he didn't know any of the people affected.

One by one the mourners filed out, some speaking softly to each other, some still weeping.

What next? Ian wondered. After a death there would be a funeral. Perhaps this one would be better attended than his parents' funeral. And perhaps this one would have food.

Jo wasn't sure what made her so uncomfortable around Frank Benson. She could understand somewhat why Ian had been uneasy around him. She didn't know, however, what exactly had prompted Ian to run away as he had.

As she turned onto the interstate ramp, she felt a chill go up her spine. She adjusted the air-conditioning vent so that it did not blow directly on her.

By the time she reached Tallahassee, she realized the car needed gasoline. The first exit had several filling stations. She chose the one that looked like it had clean restrooms.

"Well, Frank, you back to get your change from yesterday?" Lillian asked him as he sat down at the counter.

"Huh?" Frank didn't understand.

"You either forgot your change from breakfast yesterday or you've come into a pile of money and you're leaving big tips."

"I did what?"

"You left me a twenty for a five-dollar meal," Lillian explained.

"Oh, well. Keep it, Lillian. Consider it payment for some information." Lillian raised an eyebrow. "Tell me. What else did Miz Josephine Anderson find out while she was here?"

No one else came in or out of the building, at least as far as Ian could tell. George did not return as he had the afternoons before. The pastor did not come. No more people came to sit in silence. But Ian did hear Mercy and Hope meowing just behind the closed doors of the auditorium. Apparently they were hungry. Ian figured someone would come to feed them, but when a lot of time passed and the cats began to sound desperate, Ian decided to at least see what he could do.

The afternoon sun was hitting the stained-glass window just right to cast the rainbow image on the carpet. As he walked in front of the large table, Ian noticed that the image was starting to look like the shadow of something familiar. He couldn't quite make out a figure, but the pattern seemed to take shape.

Mercy and Hope bounded through the door past Ian as if he weren't even there. They ran around the room meowing wildly. Finally, they noticed Ian and both bounded back to his feet. Quickly they made a circle around him, purring and rubbing their backs on his leg. He figured they were hungry and that in the events of the baby's death, someone had forgotten to feed them. Slowly he opened the doors to the auditorium again and listened. The cats slipped by him and bolted down the stairs, still crying for food.

Ian peeked around the doorframe at the bottom of the stairs. The cats were standing at the door of the pantry where he had hidden before. Then he remembered the day he had sought refuge there when he first arrived. Mercy and Hope had wanted to share his closet hiding place, he had thought, until he realized that their food was probably kept in there.

When he opened the pantry, the cats went directly to the bag of dry cat food that sat on the bottom shelf. That was what they wanted, he figured, and he poured each of them a mound on the floor of the kitchen. As the cats ate, oblivious to his presence, Ian thought about his dream. It disturbed him still. He hadn't wanted to think about a fire ever again, but the image of the dream wouldn't go away.

Fire, fire/It just gets higher/Flame, flame/I'm to blame. Shame! Shame! /I'm to blame!

The cats had eaten their fill, but still they cried. Ian couldn't imagine what they wanted. He was a little annoyed at their persistence. They both began to pace in front of the refrigerator. *Milk,* he thought.

"OK, just a minute." Ian said, surprised to hear his own voice after so long a silence.

There was a car in Jo's driveway when she arrived. Three of her dear friends were standing on her porch, each with a casserole dish in hand.

"Where in the blue-eyed world have you been?" Eloise chided her.

"Yeah, honey. We've been calling and got no answer," Jean chimed in.

"I told the Willises next door I'd be gone for a couple of days," Jo said, trying to ward off more admonishments.

"We know that," Clara said, "but Ann said you said you'd be back yesterday and you weren't."

"No, I said I'd be back in a couple of days. I didn't say exactly when I'd be back." Jo unlocked her front door and let the casserole bearers pass.

"Well, where'd you go anyway? Why didn't you tell us? You've got no business, a woman your age, going off like that." The ladies began to set the table as they each gave their opinions about Jo's exploration.

Jo tried to be calm and patient. After all, they were her friends who were concerned about her and her safety.

"No word, deary, on Ian, according to the sheriff's office. I've been checking on the investigation for you, in your absence," Clara said.

"I've been checking on it myself, Clara. I've called several times since I left. I haven't found out his whereabouts either, but I've got a plan." Jo began to tell the ladies just how they could be the most help to her.

Chapter Twelve

Ian woke up early

to the sounds of people milling around. He wondered even before he looked if they were there for another time of silence, maybe for the pastor's wife. But these people were busy bringing in flower wreaths, potted plants, and baskets of cut flowers. Before long, Ian could detect the familiar smell of the sprays on his parents' caskets. This was probably a funeral, the baby's funeral.

Two rows of benches on either side of the aisle were marked "reserved for family." Ian thought that the pastor and his wife must have lots of family, and he thought about Aunt Jo for the first time in a while. He realized she was his only family, as far as he knew, and that if he died his aunt wouldn't need much space reserved for her. However, he wasn't sure she would even attend his funeral. He had left her, after all. Maybe she didn't care anymore. He wouldn't blame her, really. But then again, she had talked to that man at her house that day. Ian wondered how much she had told that man, or how much that man already knew. He wondered if they were working together, conspiring to place the blame on him, thinking of ways to punish him. But maybe he deserved to be punished. Maybe he was guilty of killing his only family.

Shame, shame/I'm to blame.

The phone rang at seven o'clock, but Jo had already been up for an hour making her list.

It was Jean. "Honey, I got a call from Sue Ellen," Jean said excitedly.

"Who?" Jo was a little annoyed.

"My friend, Sue Ellen, in Mobile. You remember her. She was a Phi Mu at Montevallo with me." Jo didn't remember her, but Jean went on anyway. "Well, Sue Ellen wanted us to come visit her next week in her new house in Point Clear," Jean drawled.

"Where? No, it doesn't matter. Jean, I can't go off somewhere right now. I've got to find Ian," Jo said firmly.

"I know that, honey, but I just thought you could use a little diversion, that's all."

"Jean, I really appreciate the offer, but . . ."

"Now, Josephine, you need to get away. You look so tired and spent. Sue Ellen has a lovely place on Mobile Bay. It's got all the modern conveniences."

Jean had been a good friend for a long time. She had stood beside her after Harlan died. So had Clara and Eloise. Jo felt a little guilty trying to dismiss Jean's generous invitation.

The black car had driven by twice in an hour. Jo was so intent on her list-making task that she hardly noticed, but when it went by the third time, she got a little concerned.

"Jean, I'll have to call you back."

Ian saw the woman come to the keyboard. He knew what to do. Quietly, he opened his door. *Oh no,* he thought. The door hinge had developed a slight squeak. There wasn't enough noise in the auditorium, he thought, to cover it. At least, he couldn't take a chance. He also couldn't chance his eardrums again. Putting his hands over his ears, just in case, Ian swished as much saliva in his mouth as he could. It was good enough for a few good spits. He would need to be a good shot, and he hoped that the squeaky hinge was one he could reach. Bingo! The spit wad was on target and the door opened silently, enough for him to squeeze through. And just in time too, for the musical monster started to roar just as he closed the door.

Ian had learned his spit trick on school mornings when he had to get up early to meet the bus. He never set an alarm clock because he knew what would happen if his father was awakened at that hour. It was too early for the alcohol to have worn off from the night before, and Ian had been frightened when his father ranted and raved with a hangover. Ian had trained himself to wake up precisely at 6:00 and start preparing himself and his breakfast. On one or two cold mornings, the door to his bedroom had started to squeak and he had resorted to a saliva fix. Now he was thankful that his experience had paid off.

He couldn't see anything going on from behind the door, but judging from the occasional sobs that he heard coming from the room, he figured that the funeral was about to begin. He wondered if the pastor would officiate at his own son's service.

The music stopped and Ian listened. He didn't dare try to re-enter his room. He was afraid of the lady at the keyboard. The voice of a man started, but it wasn't the voice of the pastor he knew. This voice sounded older.

"Lord, thou hast been our dwelling place in all generations. Before the mountains were brought forth, or ever thou hadst formed the earth and the world, even from everlasting to everlasting, thou art God." Ian liked the sound. It was like poetry.

"For a thousand years in thy sight are but as yesterday when it is past, and as a watch in the night," the old voice continued. "So teach us to number our days, that we may apply our hearts unto wisdom. Let not your heart be troubled: ye believe in God, believe also in me." Ian recognized this, but from where? "In my Father's house are many mansions: if it were not so, I would have told you. I go to prepare a place for you. And if I go and prepare a place for you, I will come again, and receive you unto myself; that where I am, there ye may be also." The speaker seemed to embrace these words as he spoke them. "I will not leave you comfortless: I will come to you."

Suddenly Ian recognized these words. Though he had tuned them out somewhat before, these were words spoken by the pastor at his parents' grave. Ian placed his hands over his ears again, hoping that the pastor would not speak of ashes and dust.

Finally, the music began again. The singer had a lovely voice, he thought. Not harsh like the voice of the woman who sang at the Lanes' service. This one was higher and younger sounding. Even in the hallway, he could hear it, but not the lyrics so much. He wished he could have heard how they rhymed.

✦ ✦ ✦

"Oh, hello, Miz Anderson," the syrupy voice of the sheriff answered. "What's on your mind?"

Jo hated the condescending voice he used when he talked to her, as if she were some kind of mental case. She hated to be pitied.

Jo tried to be calm and polite, but her voice had a bit of an edge to it.

"Sheriff, I need your help," Jo continued.

"I know, ma'am, and we're doing all we can to find that little runaway. We're lookin' for 'im high and low," the sheriff schmoozed.

"That's not what I'm calling about. I know you haven't found . . . and his name is Ian . . . but I'd like to ask for somebody to come over here. I feel like I'm being stalked or something." Even to Jo it sounded ridiculous.

"Stalked?"

"Yes, there is a man named Frank Benson who keeps riding by my house, three times in an hour. At least it looks like his car."

"Who is this Frank Benson, Miz Anderson?"

"He's . . . he's . . . an insurance agent from Madison. He's been here a couple of times asking questions about the fire. He wanted to talk to Ian . . . and that's probably why Ian ran. And then I was in Madison yesterday and he came to my motel room, and . . ."

"Miz Anderson, I cain't drop what I'm doing and investigate the alleged comings and goings of an old friend of yours . . ."

"Old friend? He's not an old friend, Sheriff." Jo was trying not to sound hysterical. "I have this feeling about him. I think Ian did too . . ."

Jo could hear the sheriff talking to somebody else in the room. Apparently he wasn't even listening to her. It was hard to keep her temper from being unleashed on the pompous lawman. She slammed down the phone and cried out a prayer to God for restraint. She also cried out a vow to not vote for that sheriff in the next election.

She looked out the window again and didn't see the black car anywhere. A chill ran up her spine. She pulled her cotton shawl around her shoulders and went back to writing.

When the doorbell rang, she nearly jumped out of her skin. Then she sat perfectly still and tried to think whether to pick up the phone again and call for help or just go to the door with her kitchen knife in her pocket.

"How do, ma'am." The young policeman smiled and removed his cap when she looked out the front door glass. "It's Hank Thomas from the city police. The sheriff dispatched us to come out here and check on you." Jo relaxed just a bit, but she didn't take her hand off the kitchen knife.

"I'm fine, Officer. Thank you for coming by." Jo spoke loudly and didn't open the door.

"Good, ma'am. Sheriff's office sort of turns over these kinds of cases to us on the city force."

"Hank?" Jo suddenly recognized the voice.

"Yes, ma'am. It's Hank Thomas," he answered.

Jo unlocked the dead bolt and the chain and gladly greeted the officer. "I'm sorry, Hank, I guess I'm just a little shaky right now. Didn't recognize you at first. Why, I've known you all your life. Taught you in fourth-grade Sunday school."

"Yes, ma'am."

The color was starting to come back to her face. She invited the young man to come into her front room. Being the true Southern lady, she offered him food, water, lemonade. He declined them all.

"Sure am sorry about Ian, Miz Anderson." Hank had turned out to be such a handsome young man.

"Thank you, Hank. I just don't think that the sheriff is doing enough to find him. I want them to extend the search past the Florida line and get the word out over in Alabama and Georgia. There's no telling where a resourceful boy like Ian could be hiding."

"Resourceful?" Hank asked, and Jo told the young man about Ian's past.

"So you see, I think Ian could be somewhere out there afraid to come back." Jo was trying to keep her tears in check.

"Well, Miz Anderson, what can I do to help?" Hank asked. Jo was praising God for sending him to her.

"Hank, you know Jean Mayer, from church," Jo began.

"Uh-huh."

"Well, she has a friend, Sue Ellen, in Mobile who has a son who's a lawyer, and she said she'd ask Sue Ellen to ask her son to help get the official word out." Jo was hoping she had said all that right.

"It's been on TV over there; those who get the Pensacola stations have seen his picture. Also the sheriff told me they had put the boy's information on websites and reports that go all over the country," said Hank.

"Yes, but is that enough?" Jo was hoping that Hank could pull some strings.

Hank raised an eyebrow and thought for a second. "Maybe not. I'll talk to my chief. Mind you, my jurisdiction doesn't go past the city limits of Crestview, but I think the chief has some friends in higher places over there."

"Thank you, Hank. Thank you so much." Jo extended

her hand to the young man, who grabbed it gently.

"Oh, you're welcome, Miz Anderson. Anything for you," he told her.

As Hank's cruiser drove off, she forgot for a minute about the black-car stalker. In fact, she had forgotten to even mention it again to Hank. She started to flag Hank down, but she was afraid that the man in the black car would . . . *Oh, wait, there's the black car again, and that's not Frank Benson,* she discovered. The car was driven by a man she knew who was a real estate agent and was showing houses in the area. Jo felt foolish. But she was determined to find Ian.

Ian was sad the rest of the day. Even though he didn't really know Pastor Jim or his family, he still felt sorry for him. *Babies aren't supposed to die,* he thought. *Neither are parents.*

As soon as the funeral party left the building, George came in to clean. He didn't whistle this time but went about his work slowly and deliberately. Ian could tell that the old man felt the sorrow of the moment too.

Ian waited until George was through and had slammed the downstairs door shut. Then Ian went for a lazy float in his private pool.

Jo hadn't expected to hear from Hank so soon. But he called before two hours had passed with some encouraging news.

"Miz Anderson, the chief talked to some buddies over

on the Mobile County police force to see what they could do. The officer over there said he could get a man in their department to ask around. He said it was kind of quiet around there and that he'd be glad to see what he could do. Said he'd seen Ian's picture on TV."

Jo couldn't help but cry. "Bless you, Hank."

"I'll keep you updated on the slightest whisper about this, OK?" the kind officer said.

Jo hung up the phone and, for the first time in a while, dropped to her knees and thanked God for this tiny bit of progress. She didn't want to sound ungrateful, but she expanded her prayer to ask for more, more information that would lead them to Ian.

Ian waited until it was completely dark before he went downstairs. There were no sounds at all anywhere, and so he wasn't even too careful walking down the steps.

He was right about the food. There was even more in the refrigerator than there had been before. He had heard that people brought food when somebody died. Though he didn't wish death on anybody, this fact might be crucial to his survival.

The first thing Ian saw were pies, the kind he had seen in the bakery window next door. The first one had been sliced already. Chocolate with a thick meringue. Sugar beads had formed on the fluffy, white topping. He couldn't even remember the last time he had had pie. But before he'd slice off a sliver for himself, he knew he must eat something "nutritious" like meat or vegetables. There was bread also. He didn't even take the time to ration out and tamp down from the bowls and platters. He just lifted the plastic wrap and took spoonfuls of corn and peas and then reached for double handfuls of turkey. He was careful, though, not to take so much as to not enjoy the pie that he would surely eat. Cold milk in the refrigerator door washed it all down. Ian patted his stomach and thought how strange it felt to be full. It had been so long. He ate another sliver of pie to celebrate.

Ian froze when he heard the cats outside the basement door. He was afraid that Pastor Jim or George accompanied them. He stepped inside the pantry with a fork still in his hand. Listening. The cats continued to meow. Finally, Ian stepped out of the pantry and went to the door. He opened it ever so slightly to let the cats through, and then he realized that this was the first time he had actually seen outside in several days. Even though it was pitch-dark and he was peering into a smelly alleyway, he still savored the connection with the world for just a moment. Suddenly something shuffled. Quickly he closed the door and locked it. Retreating back to the pantry, he realized he was holed up again in the hiding place with Mercy and Hope, who were crying incessantly for food.

This could be it, Ian thought to himself. He knew that his asylum would not last for long. Either he would leave enough clues that he'd have to seek another refuge or else someone would find him and return him to Aunt Jo. Neither option sounded safe to him. He felt around in the dark closet for the cat food. It was right where he had left it last time. He opened the bag, pulled out a handful of dry pieces, and held it down for the cats to eat. Their furry mouths tickled his hand, and he had to force himself not to laugh out loud. The cats purred and licked Ian's empty hand. The wet barbs on their tongues felt odd. He felt a little guilty feeding them dry food from a bag when his belly was so full of the best food he'd ever tasted.

Frank got home about dawn. He was exhausted, but he was too troubled to sleep. He figured he'd wait for a couple of hours before he called his father at the lake. He dreaded telling him all that had happened with the fire, the boy's disappearance, and the aunt's tireless search for him.

Chapter Thirteen

Dad, it's me, Frank.

He suddenly realized he hadn't needed to wait until eight o'clock to call his father. The older Benson usually rose at dawn and got in a couple of hours of fishing before it got too hot on the lake. Even in late May, the heat and humidity were fierce, and it would be unbearable in a month.

Charles Benson was a self-made millionaire, one of only three or four in Madison. When he retired from the insurance and real estate business, he had never missed the daily grind of running his own business.

With his brother Anthony being the "front man" as they called him, Charles had been left with the bookkeeping, the personnel details, and the paperwork. It was tedious. It was hard work, and Charles had always felt a bit put out poring over the mundane while his brother took clients fishing and golfing. But Anthony had had the more gregarious personality and not much of an eye for detail. In fact, early on in the business, Anthony had listed several properties and sold several policies with just verbal agreements. He had figured that the handshake of a friend was contract enough. Charles had hit the roof. He had had to backtrack and run paperwork on all the transactions, holding his breath all the while that they didn't get sued or stuck with some arrangement that Anthony had promised without checking out its feasibility.

Charles and Anthony had finally agreed that Charles was the more businesslike of the two and should, therefore, fall into the role of comptroller. Anthony would be the outside salesman, an arrangement that left Charles a little more haggard for his years. Gin and tonic had become his favorite sedative. After retirement, Charles did not substitute fishing for drinking, however. He merely added it to his relaxation techniques.

When Charles answered the phone, he was already into his second Alabama Slammer.

Jim was glad to see Abbie eating a little breakfast when he entered her hospital room. She looked so weak. Her hand shook as she tried to scoop scrambled eggs onto her fork.

"Here, honey, let me help you," Jim insisted.

Already the swelling was going down and her face had shrunk almost to its original size, but her eyes were distant and sunken. Jim did not even know how to talk about the baby. The grief was so new and deep that even he didn't know how to deal with it.

The doctor had told Jim that Abbie's condition was improving daily and that giving birth is the only way to treat severe eclampsia and save the mother and hopefully the baby as well. The results were not always as disastrous as theirs had been. Many preterm babies were delivered safely to save the mother, but without serious complications. However, little James's lungs had been so underdeveloped that even the latest neonatal techniques could not save him.

Abbie leaned back against her pillow after two bites. Jim was grateful that she was going to be all right, but he had no idea how they would deal with it all emotionally.

"I brought you a clean nightgown," Jim said, trying to start a conversation.

"Thank you," Abbie said weakly.

"So many people have called and come by and sent cards and flowers and letters." Jim was trying hard to be strong for her sake.

"Good."

"Your mom and dad will be here soon. I told them to get as much sleep as they could this morning."

"OK."

"Do you want me to open the window, honey? It's a nice day," Jim was trying to make this a normal visit.

Suddenly Abbie spoke in a hollow tone. "I can't cry," she said. Jim turned from the window blinds and was actually frightened by the look on his wife's face. He didn't know what to say. He had cried buckets already, most of them in anger. The sight of that tiny white casket sitting under the pulpit he preached from every Sunday tore his heart out.

At first he had tried to hold back the tears, to be strong in front of his congregation, but he couldn't help it. Even the voice of his beloved mentor and former seminary professor who graciously officiated at the funeral could not comfort him. The passage from First Corinthians was so familiar to him. He had read and studied it countless times. "O death, where is thy sting? O grave, where is thy victory?

. . . Thanks be to God, which giveth us the victory through our Lord Jesus Christ." But Jim had felt no victory. Death had defeated him and his dream of having a son. And perhaps stinging death might swallow even his beloved Abbie. No, he could not hold back the angry tears. And as he had wailed, the sweet people around him shared his grief.

"I know . . ." Jim's voice trailed off as he stared out the window.

"Was it a nice funeral?" Abbie's tone was stilted and cool.

"Yeah," Jim answered, holding back a sob.

"Good." And Abbie closed her eyes and fell asleep.

The taste of the outdoors he had had the night before made Ian long for more. He knew he couldn't go out in the daytime at all, but he was getting stir-crazy inside his little perch;, and the more he thought about it, the more he was determined to venture outside that night. Ian wondered if there was another exit other than the one in the basement that went out to the alley and the one on the front of the building. He would have to explore his space a little more widely. In the meantime, he settled in to read through a stack of books he had found in one of the rooms he had seen before, the room with small chairs and tables. Most of the books looked way below his reading level, but at least they would pass the time until dark.

Jo welcomed Hank Thomas at her door with a smile. She was so proud of him and so grateful for his kind attention.

"Please, Hank, come in and let me fix you something." Jo went about pouring coffee and setting a plate on the table before even hearing Hank's response.

"Now, Miz Anderson, I can't stay long. I'm about to go on duty, and I thought I'd stop by and tell you what I found on the FCIC database," Hank said, looking longingly at the piping hot coffee.

"The data what?"

"Database, ma'am. It's the Florida Crime Investigation Center system where we can access information on our computers about investigations, past cases, things like that." Hank found himself sitting down to a plate of homemade biscuits and pear preserves.

"Uh-huh." Jo didn't really understand.

"There wasn't much there at first, but then I dug a little deeper. I researched that name you gave the sheriff: Frank Benson," Hank continued, and Jo started to listen.

"Uh huh."

"Well, I didn't find a thing about him in our files."

"So, you think I'm wrong about him and shouldn't be so paranoid," Jo said.

"I didn't say that, Miz Anderson. I said I didn't find anything on Frank Benson from Madison, Florida, but his father, Charles Benson—now that's another story."

Jo sat down next to Hank and listened intently.

Hank stuffed two biscuits with preserves and butter, but before he took a bite he said, "Seems Mr. Benson, the senior, had a little auto accident almost ten years ago. Totaled his Cadillac but didn't hurt him at all."

Jo didn't know what all this had to do with Ian, but she let Hank continue.

"Seems Mr. Benson was driving on the wrong side of the road one night and hit another car, driven by . . . Ed Lane."

"What?" Jo's jaw dropped. Hank let the news sink in. Taking advantage of the pause, he took a large bite of biscuit.

"Oh, these are good, Miz Anderson," Hank said, wiping his chin. "No charges were ever filed by Ed, and the police report just lists it as an accident."

"So, how do you know Charles Benson was driving on the wrong side of the road?"

"Eyewitness," Hank answered between bites and gulps of coffee.

"Who?"

"Mary Lane, Ian's mother."

"Mary saw the whole thing?"

"She was in the car. So was Ian in an infant seat. Neither of them was hurt."

"Why didn't she go to the police? Why didn't she tell somebody that the other guy caused the accident?" Jo was too curious to notice Hank's coffee cup was empty.

"Well, I don't know, except did you ever wonder how your niece and nephew survived on a disability check? He hadn't worked in years. And have you wondered where that house they lived in came from? Apparently, it was a pretty nice house, and well insured. That's why social services never found the place unfit for a child. And did you wonder about the insurance money?" Hank got up to refill his cup.

"How do you know all this?"

"Well, I have a cousin in Madison who used to be friends with the officer on the scene of the accident."

"Used to be?"

"Yeah, he's no longer with the force. In fact, my cousin says he moved out of Madison shortly after the accident. But not before he told his best friend what he saw."

"His best friend was your cousin?"

Hank nodded.

"How do you know about the insurance money, Hank?" Hank got up to refill his cup. Jo was a little embarrassed that a guest in her house would have to serve himself, but she was too distracted to care.

"Well, my cousin knows somebody who works for the Benson company. And she files the claims and . . ."

"Oh, Hank Thomas, you and your cousin are better than Magnum P.I."

"My cousin probably knows more than he's telling me, and he was terrified to tell me what he did."

"Maybe Frank Benson, or at least his father, was paying Ed and Mary to keep quiet. You think old man Benson was drinking and driving that night or something and Mary knew it and . . . ?"

"Rumor has it the old man is a lush. After the accident, he hired a driver so he could keep the juice flowing without endangering himself or others." Hank finished off the last bite of biscuit.

"That was nice of him," Jo said sarcastically. She was intrigued by the news, but she had to ask. "But really, what does this have to do with Ian? I mean, he's still missing and the longer we wait . . ."

"That's what concerns me, Miz Anderson," Hank leaned his elbows on the table and raised his coffee cup to his lips. "You told me that the bank teller said Ian cashed some of his parents' checks there, didn't you? I'm afraid that Frank Benson may have had something to do with the Lanes' death and that he may be wanting to find Ian to make sure he doesn't know something about the arrangement his own father had with Ian's father."

The thought made Jo's heart sink. Not only was he in danger of starving or being hurt by the elements, but now perhaps the boy was being chased by a killer.

"Well, we've got to do something, Hank," Jo said as she stood and started pacing.

"Yeah, we do, Miz Anderson, and I'll be glad to help you any way I can." Hank stood also and put his dishes in the sink. "I told you our chief had connections with Mobile law enforcement. He's got somebody out looking for Ian right now. They're starting with hospitals and morgues."

Jo started to protest.

"Now, Miz Anderson, that's procedure. But their next move is to start searching the streets. Between us here in Florida and them over there in south Alabama, we'll check everywhere a little boy can be," Hank said. "They're also gonna put his face on the Mobile stations, and some of them can be picked up as far as Louisiana."

Jo hugged the big police officer around the waist. Hank put his hands gently around his old Sunday school teacher.

"I can't thank you enough." Jo began to cry.

"Oh, Miz Anderson, I'm glad to help. You did a lot for me. If you remember, you did more for me than I could ever do for you."

Jo looked up at him. She didn't understand.

Gently he looked down at the older woman and said, "Remember, you led me to Christ."

George made his afternoon cleaning visit. It didn't take very long since he had just cleaned after the funeral. Ian heard him downstairs banging around in the kitchen, and then he heard the cats meowing. George spoke to them gruffly. Soon the cats stopped meowing. Ian figured that George had either fed them or had shooed them out into the alley or both. Either way, within a few minutes the basement door slammed shut and the building was silent.

Ian didn't want to wait until it was completely dark to find another exit. Around dusk, he descended the steps from his suite and, instead of following the usual hallway that led off to the auditorium, he followed the steps that led to his right. There were five steps to a landing, then ten or so more to another landing, then a dead end. There it was to the left! A door to the outside.

Ian looked out. He was excited at what he saw. There was a playground! Well, just an old swing set enclosed by a chain-link fence. There were no children around at all. In fact, it didn't look like the swings had been used very recently. Short weeds grew around the base of the fence and under the swing. Ian made a mental note to himself to not tamp down the weeds too much if he decided to play in the yard after dark.

Behind the playground, toward the back of the main building, was a grassy spot with two large shade trees in the middle. A heavy iron gate surrounded it all. The trees looked too high for Ian to climb, but he thought that the grassy spot might be a nice place to sit and look out at the world. But as Ian looked closer, he could tell that this was not just an open space. There were gray tablets sticking up in the earth, and on the far side of the spot, there were colorful flowers. Some of the flowers were lying down and others were propped up on metal stands. Ian didn't have to wonder what this was. He had seen a cemetery before. He wondered, then, if the fresh flowers were on a fresh grave, perhaps the little baby's grave.

Ian wasn't sure he wanted to come back to the cemetery during his after-dark outings, but he would surely visit the playground.

Just as Ian was about to turn to ascend the stairs, a figure crossed in front of him. Ian quickly hid from plain view. He thought, at first, that it was George cleaning up the grounds around the place. But then he realized this was not George but Pastor Jim instead. Ian knew he had been right, that the new grave was where the baby had been buried. Ian watched in sadness as the young father opened the iron gate, walked slowly to the graveside, and dropped to his knees. It looked as though the pastor was weeping and talking to someone at the same time. Ian had learned that this could be when Pastor Jim talks to God. Ian wondered what a man could say to God at a time like this, and though he couldn't hear them, Ian noticed that the pastor's words seemed to be unhindered.

Jim let out a primal scream, but he didn't feel any better. "What could You have possibly sent me here for? Now I know what they mean by godforsaken. This whole place is a graveyard! A dead church, a dead son, dead everything!" Jim rambled and screamed and then sat and rocked in silence. "I want out! Out of here!" His angry tears were unashamed to fall.

For an hour, Jim tried to strip himself of the encumbrances and obligations of his calling. "You promised to bless my ministry, but instead You have cursed it! Why? Haven't I been faithful? Hasn't Abbie been faithful? Does none of that matter to You now?"

Jim's voice grew raw from the screaming and the salty tears. "I want out!"

"Walk with Me one more mile." Jim knew the voice, but he tried to block it out.

"No! I've come too far already."

"Walk with Me one more mile."

"What? What is one more mile, God? Huh? What does that mean? A day? A year? You won't even speak words that make sense," Jim strained a whisper. "I won't!"

"One more mile, Jim. Then if you want to quit, you can." These were hard, but kind words to hear.

A scene came to Jim's mind of a pastoral-counseling course he had taken in seminary. He had no idea why he suddenly thought of that class. It had just been a class! He couldn't even recall one concept, one lesson he had learned there. But then he remembered another Bible class in which they had studied messianic prophecies in the Old Testament. He had studied the list of names that Isaiah had given the coming Messiah. Wonderful Counselor. Mighty God. Everlasting Father. Prince of Peace.

Why had he recalled such images?

Wonderful Counselor. All at once the Voice and the Vision began to make their impact. The professor who taught his class had emphasized that the process of healing may be slow and painful. Many would want to quit.

Jim Copeland lay down on the fresh-dug earth of his son's grave and agreed to keep coming back to the Counselor. But one more mile. That's all he would commit to.

Chapter Fourteen

The best Ian could tell,

it was Saturday. He usually slept a little later on Saturdays, and since he had stayed up late the night before enjoying the outside playground, he decided to turn over and go back to sleep for a while.

Just as he was about to relax again, he heard Mercy and Hope downstairs in the basement. Apparently someone had let them in, and hopefully somebody was feeding them too. Ian lay awake wondering if it was George or the still-grieving Pastor Jim who had arrived early on this Saturday morning.

Ian also remembered that it was just a week before that he had found this haven, his asylum. He was thankful that he had not only survived for seven whole days on his own, but that he was clean, warm, and well fed. He was a little bit smug when he thought of the other boys his age that he knew and how they probably wouldn't have lasted a day alone, much less a week. This was certainly something to celebrate.

Just then, Ian heard a knock on a door. The sound shocked him and made him tense. The knock seemed to be coming from behind the big front doors of the building. Ian listened and waited. He heard footsteps up the stairs, a rattling of keys, and then voices.

"Hi, are you the reverend here?" a man's voice asked.

"Yes, I'm Jim Copeland, pastor of Broad Street," the pastor answered. "What can I do for you, Officer?"

Officer?

The man began to speak in a low-pitched monotone. "We just received an alert on a missing child who may or may not be in the area. Here is a picture of him."

There was a pause.

"Reverend, he ran away from his legal guardian in Crestview, Florida, over a week ago. The Florida authorities have exhausted every lead they have, and they're extending an active search across state lines. We wonder if you've seen the boy," the man asked.

"No." It was an abrupt response. There was another pause.

"All right. Well, if you'd put this picture up on a bulletin board somewhere and ask your . . . uh . . . parishioners if they've seen him, we'd appreciate it. Any information you could give us . . . well, just call the number on the flyer there."

The door closed and then came the rattle of keys.

Ian waited. He heard footsteps back down the stairs and then nothing. He thought about the officer's words. He realized then that there were people out in the world looking for him, people with uniforms and flyers. He was suddenly afraid again, afraid of what might happen to him if they found out where he was and what he'd done. He didn't know what to do, where to turn.

Burn, burn/Where to turn?/Burn, burn/Where to turn?

The rhyme in his head caught him by surprise. He hadn't thought of one for . . . well, just that once in his dream. Before that, he couldn't remember what was before that.

Burn, burn/Where to turn?/Burn, burn/Where to turn?

What a cruel irony, Jim thought as he sat in his tiny office next to the kitchen in the basement. *They're looking for a fatherless boy. I am a sonless father.* The pain of that thought pricked his soul to its deepest place, and the numbness gave way to intense anguish. He cried out to God without words or gestures. In the safety of his own asylum, he admitted that he could not and would not see God's hand in any of this. The face on the flyer looked back at him, and Jim cursed it before he threw the flyer in the trash.

"Son, what have you done about all this?" Charles Benson slurred his words.

"I've been talking to the aunt. I've even followed her around some to see if she's found anything out about the boy," Frank explained to his father.

"How long has the boy been gone?"

"Little over a week."

"How you reckon that boy got out of that burning house so quick?"

"Apparently the boy's pretty smart. He's eluding officials now in three states."

"Reckon the boy's dead?"

Frank knew that no one could hear him on his private

line, but he was still trying to talk in whispers. "Who knows? Smart as he is, he may be in Texas by now."

"And smart as he is, he probably knows our connection with his mama and daddy too."

Frank didn't like the sound of that. He had tried to dismiss the idea that Ian was on to their arrangement. But when he had actually seen the boy in Josephine Anderson's front room, he just felt as though Ian knew more than he should.

"Keep lookin', Son, and let me know what you find out," the elder man said, hanging up the phone.

Frank was glad that he knew someone in the Mobile Police Department he could count on, an old friend with a checkered past of his own.

Abbie felt better. Her head didn't ache when she sat up in bed, and she even had a little appetite. And when Jim poked his head in the door, she had enough energy to smile at him.

"Well, that's a wonderful sight," Jim said, going immediately to her side. He stroked her hair as he had every day since they'd brought her there.

"I'm sorry I haven't been much company lately." Abbie was surprised by the shakiness of her own voice.

"Don't worry about that. You just get to feeling better so I can take you home." Jim tried to sound chipper.

"Are you going visiting today?" she asked.

"No."

"It's Saturday. I imagine the kids in the housing project will wonder where you are."

"I don't care." Jim didn't mean for that to slip out.

Abbie didn't even respond. She sensed, as she always

had, when Jim was wrestling with God about something. She could tell that Jim's grief was turning into anger, and she silently prayed for God to take it away.

"I mean, it won't hurt them to miss me one Saturday. My place is here with you."

"Jim." Abbie reached out and took her husband's hand.

Jim looked at his wife, whose deep-set eyes looked like they might be too tired to see things clearly. However, Abbie had always known what to say, and when to say nothing. Tears burned behind his eyes.

"I finally had a good cry this morning," she said without much emotion. "There was the picture of a missing boy on the TV news. I remember seeing that on the Pensacola station last week. Well, anyway, I looked at that face and thought that's maybe how James would have looked in a few years, and I suddenly realized I was crying. Miraculously, no nurses came in for a while and so, Jim, I just sat here and cried. It was what I needed to get started dealing with this, I think."

Jim's tears broke through, and he lay down beside his wife and held her. She continued to talk quietly while she cried. Jim had always marveled how she could keep her voice from quivering and her nose from running profusely while she shed tears, whether of joy or sorrow. She could even sing a solo and maintain perfect tone while tears streamed down her cheeks. When he cried, though, his whole face looked as if it were on fire, and his dripping nose ran as if it were trying to put it out.

He let her talk, saying anything she wanted to say before he spoke again.

"I'm so sorry I let this happen to us," Jim finally said.

"You are not to blame, Reverend Jim Copeland," Abbie chided him.

He knew in his heart it was true, but for some reason it felt better to blame himself than to let Abbie carry any of the burden. But Jim still knew that God could have saved his son if He'd wanted to.

"One more mile," Jim heard.

Jean came by and brought lunch. Of course, Jo had already fixed fried green tomatoes and corn bread. So, the two women sat down and combined their meals and talked about Ian. Jo was hesitant to share anything about the Frank Benson case. She figured that Jean didn't need to know any of that until all the facts were in. And, besides, the whole thing would be all over town before nightfall, and Jo didn't think that was the right thing for Ian right now.

"Oh, I almost forgot," Jean said as she cut into a homemade apple tart. "Sue Ellen called me again this morning and wanted to know if we'd like to come to Point Clear tomorrow."

"We?"

"Yeah, me and you, sweetie."

Just as Jo was about to decline, Jean continued, "Sue Ellen's little pastor and his wife just lost a baby this week. They're just torn up about it. She wanted us to pray for them. She thought we'd use this time sort of as a prayer retreat—you know, like we did that time at Lake Yale. Anyway, she wants us to drive down after church tomorrow."

Jo didn't know what to say.

Jean kept talking without really waiting for Jo's response. "I told Sue Ellen I'd let her know something today."

"Well," Jo tried to figure out how to respond politely.

"My place is here, Jean, in case somebody calls about Ian." But then she remembered the cell phone she had bought right after she had gone on her fact-finding trip to Madison. She took it with her everywhere she went, just in case. "I'm afraid that far away I couldn't get cell phone service. I don't know how those things work."

Jean had an answer. "Honey, Sue Ellen uses her phone there all the time. Says she gets great reception, better than a regular phone. You know you can give the policemen that number. Now, come on, Jo. You need a break. Sue Ellen will feed us, and we can sit out on the dock and dangle our feet in the bay." Jean giggled and scrunched her nose.

Chapter Fifteen

Ian knew the routine.

It was Sunday, and even though the sun was just coming up, he was sure that the auditorium would be filling up in a few hours. He also knew that the lady at the keyboard would come in early and start practicing. He looked out into the room and watched intently, not wanting to miss her entrance.

The food stash he'd gathered the night before was piled neatly in the corner of his room, and he figured he'd need to get started on breakfast soon. There had been so much food left in the kitchen after the funeral that he felt like it would be virtually impossible to detect when something was missing. Ian had gotten a little bold and had put together a care package for himself that consisted of a small jar of home-made jelly, several pieces of bread, and a whole jug of sweetened ice tea. There had also been some individual cups of vanilla ice cream in the freezer. He knew they'd melt soon, so he helped himself to two of them right there in the kitchen. Though he was more and more certain that the food would not be missed, he was still careful to wash the utensils he used and to dispose of his trash in a way that George would not notice as out of the ordinary.

Jo got up early to read her Sunday school lesson. She usually read it on Saturdays, but the past week had been a little unusual, and she had actually forgotten it. She thought back to the week before, and even though they still hadn't found Ian, she felt more encouraged and at peace about his condition. She didn't know exactly why.

May and June were always months that brought some kind of family emphasis to her church. It usually started with Mother's Day and ended with Father's Day. Brother Brewton always seemed to think of an effective way to talk about families. He'd had to adapt a little bit over the years since there were so many more single-parent families in the church now, but somehow he managed to bring a pertinent message to everybody in the congregation, even those like her who were in unconventional families.

Jo read, "A certain man had two sons: And the younger of them said to his father, Father, give me the portion of goods that falleth to me. And he divided unto them his living. And not many days after the younger son gathered all together, and took his journey into a far country, and there wasted his substance with riotous living."

Jo loved the story of the prodigal son. Though the parable was about a family, a man and his two sons, Jo knew that Jesus had told it to show, by using a common example the people could understand, a glimpse into the heavenly Father's heart of love.

She closed the Bible and thanked God for loving her. She then asked the Father to bring her prodigal boy home safely.

Ian realized he must have dozed off again. When he woke up his arm was numb. He slung it around a bit to get the feeling back. Looking out into the auditorium, still empty of people, the morning sun caught the stained-glass window just right. Although it didn't put the rainbow of color on the carpet at that hour, its picture was very clear. The mosaic created a pattern too that seemed familiar.

Ian looked back through the books he'd found. Finally, he turned to a picture with a striking resemblance to the glass image. Underneath the picture, the caption was "Jesus said, I am the Good Shepherd." The Man in the picture was obviously the Man they called Jesus. Even though Ian didn't understand what it meant, looking up at the window made him feel safe.

The door slung open and morning light streamed in, casting the man's shadow on the aisle carpet. It was Pastor Jim.

Ian was interested to see what he would do, if he would lie in front of the stage as before and cry and mumble to God. The pastor did not lie facedown, but he did walk slowly to the front bench and sit down. He looked exhausted.

"I'm so tired, Lord. The last mile has completely drained me . . . but I'm still here. OK, I'll go another mile. Maybe the next one won't be so hard. God, it still hurts so bad." The man paused and took a deep tearful breath. Then there was silence.

"God, I guess You know what it's like to give up a Son,

so You know what I'm going through. You have felt what I feel. I just wanted to hold on to little James, to not let him go, and then I've been blaming You for taking him away. I'm sorry." And the man went silent. He sat motionless for what seemed like forever.

Ian didn't move. He watched the man and he watched how the sun shifted slightly, moving the shadows, moving the image, projecting perfectly the Good Shepherd over the man. Something in Ian's heart broke loose, and he started to cry. He didn't know why, but suddenly he wanted to be embraced by strong, loving arms.

Ian would sit in the hallway outside his closed door while the music played during the church service, but he would crawl quietly back into his room to watch and listen to what the young pastor would say to the people.

But instead, the same older man who had presided over the impromptu prayer service earlier in the week spoke to the congregation.

"Brother Jim isn't here this morning. Under the circumstances, I think we all understand why. I mean, we shouldn't presume upon Brother Jim to preach to us in light of the tragedy of this week. We will, however, have a time of intercession for him and Abbie. As the organist plays quietly, will you please lift your hearts in prayer for this, our dear brother and sister . . ."

The man stopped abruptly and looked at the double doors where his young pastor stood. The congregation turned.

"Pastor . . ."

"Thank you, Raymond. Thank you all so much. Sorry I'm late," Jim said. The older man smiled and sat down on the front row. The pastor walked slowly down the center aisle, reading from the book as he went.

"And the Lord struck the child that Uriah's wife bare unto David, and it was very sick. David therefore besought God for the child; and David fasted, and went in, and lay all night upon the earth."

Ian did not know this person named David, but it sounded like a good story, so he listened intently.

"And it came to pass on the seventh day, that the child died."

Already several people in the crowd had tears in their eyes.

The pastor continued to read as he climbed the steps to the pulpit. "Then David arose from the earth, and washed, and anointed himself, and changed his apparel, and came into the house of the Lord, and worshiped."

Jim Copeland looked up from the reading; he laid the Bible on the stand. Though he looked thin and tired, he was clean and wearing his best suit. Leaning both arms on the pulpit, he gave a sly smile and said, "Abbie says I should join the WWF. She says I wrestle with God so much that she's sure I could do well on the pro tour." The congregation laughed and wiped their tears.

"The events of this last week have been the worst I've ever been through. I went from scared, to shock, to panic, to . . . angry. And then the story in Second Samuel came to my mind. I remember David's pain at losing a newborn son. While the son lived, he fasted, he prayed, he called out to God. God did hear David's prayer, but He did not see fit to grant it. After the child died, David showered and shaved, ate a meal, and worshiped God. He didn't blame God. He worshiped God. That's what I've come here today to do. Well, also to thank you all for your kindness and care of me and Abbie, but mostly . . . to worship."

Jim looked up and asked, "Will you worship with me?"

And he began to hum, a tune that Ian recognized. The same man had hummed the same tune on the night he hid himself in the pantry. Ian was curious how the words went. Some of the other people began to hum with the man, and soon everyone in the room seemed to be singing together.

"Jesus, Jesus, how I trust Him! How I've proved Him o'er and o'er. Jesus, Jesus, precious Jesus! O for grace to trust Him more!" Ian liked the rhyme, but even more he liked the sound of the people singing the words together. And they all seemed to believe what they sang, that this Jesus could be trusted.

At the end of the song, a man in a police uniform came through the door and sat on the back row. Ian felt fear rise up in him at the sight of the officer.

The pastor prayed out loud for a long time, and the rest of the people closed their eyes. Some came to the front of the room and kneeled down. Some leaned their heads on the row in front of them. Others even talked softly out loud, but all looked as if they were talking to God too. Ian had never talked to God himself. *I wouldn't even know how to,* he thought. But he wondered if he might try it and ask Him to help him not be afraid, for that was all Ian could think of to say.

"In Jesus' name. Amen," the prayer ended, and people went back to their seats.

After a short but heartfelt sermon, Pastor Jim took a crumpled piece of paper out of his pocket, smoothed it a bit, and looked at the crowd.

"Officer Mixon tells me that citizen involvement is the best way to solve a case. You may have seen the picture on the TV news of a runaway boy."

Ian's face flushed.

"He ran away from his guardian in the Panhandle of

Florida. Officials have no leads at this point and have no reason to believe that he is in Mobile. However, Officer Mixon has so graciously agreed to pass out flyers with the boy's picture on it." Jim gestured to the policeman sitting on the back row. The crowd turned and looked. "Please take one, and let's help find this lost child. If you have any information about him, there is a number on the flyer to call." Many in the congregation nodded to each other, vowing to join the search.

Jim continued. "Now I hope you don't think it rude if I 'preach and run,' but I'd like to get back to the hospital by noon to eat with Abbie, so if you'd forgive me for taking off and not greeting you at the door . . ."

The congregation smiled as if they understood perfectly.

As Jim walked out the door, he added, "Please keep praying for us . . . and don't forget to help with any information about that boy."

Ian was stunned. The world was definitely looking for him now. Should he lie low? Should he move on? Should he even turn himself in? The thought so troubled him that he failed to see the lady come to the keyboard.

Man! The sound almost knocked him backward. Covering his ears, he crawled under his thin mattress and prayed for the sound to stop.

✦ ✦ ✦

Frank caught his old buddy, Pete Lambert, at home drinking his coffee and reading the Sunday paper.

"Pete!" Frank said in his good-ol'-boy voice when the man answered the phone.

"Repeat!" Pete knew exactly who it was, an old friend he'd known for years. Pete and Frank had been such good friends as kids that they were called Pete and Repeat. It had been endearing at the time.

"Hey, keepin' Mobile streets clean?" Frank asked. He was referring to his friend's job on the police force keeping the city of Mobile crime free.

"You know it, buddy, you know it!"

"Heard you made looey, man," Frank said, having heard about Pete's promotion to lieutenant.

"Yeah, how 'bout that? They're pretty desperate over here," Pete answered. "How're you doin'?"

"Good, good. Busy." A few more niceties were exchanged about family and mutual friends. "Say, have y'all got a case going on a runaway boy from the Panhandle?" Frank asked almost as an aside.

"Yeah. Got a sergeant who's a family man and has sorta taken this on as a project. Don't know a thing about it much. No sightings over here, but for some reason the boy's guardian thinks he may have crossed the state line. It'd be easier for somebody to get lost in a city like Mobile. Lots of nooks and crannies to hide in."

"What do you think?" Frank asked.

"No idea. Kid could be anywhere. Why?" Pete asked.

"Well, he was one of my clients. Ah, his parents were, actually, and I was just concerned about 'im. Thought you might know something."

"No. Nothing yet, but I'll ask tomorrow if the sergeant's got anything. Hey, you still got that bass boat?"

"My dad's got it at Seminole. I go up there ever' now and then and we go out." Frank was glad to change the subject for a while.

"Well, conditions are getting right for a Jubilee. Why don't you come over in a few weeks when they're predicting one, and we'll go out to the point and net some blue crab and flounder? Oughta be fun." The invitation was always open, Frank knew, to take part in the summer activity on the bay when fish and other sea life came near shore to swim lazily on the surface searching for oxygen. It would be in the predawn hours, when conditions were right, that these creatures could be easily caught, even with bare hands.

"Sounds good, bro. But let me know the minute you hear about this boy. I'm real worried about 'im. I got to know his parents real well before they were killed tragically in a fire." Frank tried to conjure up a tearful tone.

Pete vowed to call as soon as he heard anything about the boy.

Chapter Sixteen

He smelled the cigarette

odor a split second before he felt the hand on his shoulder. Ian didn't even freeze or turn to see who had grabbed him. He just ran headlong out of the fenced playground, past the cemetery, and into an open field of weeds and broken concrete.

Ahead, high above him, a busy highway stretched out both ways into the night. Ian thought at first that it might be his path to freedom. But wait, he hadn't really wanted his freedom, had he? He had sought, and had found, a safe house. Now he was running away from it. No, he was running away from somebody who had approached him while he played, apparently moving in on him so silently that he didn't even notice. Ian was too confused to run and too scared to retreat, and so he dropped down into the weeds and listened to his own heartbeat pounding in his ears. He could hear no footsteps, no one following him.

After about a minute, he could hear the sound of traffic

on the raised highway and on another street that ran under it. *Where can I go?* Ian thought. He recognized his question as the same one the pastor had spoken once in his conversations with God.

This would be his prayer, then, the third one in his life, the third one in a day.

He looked up and saw a large cement tube maybe fifty yards away. Crawling inside, he leaned against the side and tried to catch his breath.

His first human contact in over a week, and it frightened him almost to death. Who was the person? What was his intention? Did he recognize Ian, and would the person have done him harm?

Ian listened again for footsteps. There were none. He definitely had not been chased or followed, it seemed, and he tried to regulate his breathing so that he could remain totally quiet, just in case.

Sue Ellen had welcomed her old friend Jean and her new friend Jo to her new home with a dinner of Cajun shrimp, beans, and rice. "Mobile is said to be a little New Orleans," Sue Ellen had told the ladies.

Jo was not used to the spicy seasoning, and as she later lay on the lumpy mattress of a sofa bed, she wondered why she was even there. She thought that she should be at home in case someone from the sheriff's department or state police called with information about Ian. Jo felt around in the semi-dark for her cell phone. It was on and fully charged. Jo had been gone for almost twelve hours and so far, nothing. Worry, Cajun seasoning, and a bad mattress kept Jo awake until well after midnight. In fact, she was afraid she'd never get to sleep at all. She prayed, "Oh, Lord, let me sleep, but more than that, let Ian sleep in Your arms of safety."

At three A.M., she awoke and prayed the prayer again.

Mercy and Hope meowed nearby. The sound resonated. It echoed strangely. Ian thought without opening his eyes that it sounded like he was in the belly of the great fish the pastor had talked about. Ian breathed in. The smell was not of worms, seaweed, and dead fish. He opened his eyes and realized that he was still in a concrete tunnel. Ian pulled himself up on his elbow and looked around. *I'm on the run from being on the run,* Ian thought.

"Here, kitty," Ian called to the cats. His own voice echoed inside the tube. The cats ran to his side and arched their backs as Ian rubbed them. They purred and rubbed against the boy.

It was still dark outside, but Ian could hear the pre-dawn roar of traffic on the highway. He realized that he had to get back to the church building before the sun came up, or he'd have to wait until dark again. He couldn't imagine sitting inside the pipe all day long.

Slowly Ian crawled to the end of the pipe and peeked out. He stood up and looked toward the building to see if there was anyone there. The church building looked different on the outside and from a distance. From the new view with only a half-moon and street-lights, Ian thought that the place looked a lot more run-down. The style was definitely outdated, and it looked like the paint on the eaves was peeling. The landscaping was sparse but neatly trimmed. The property was surrounded on three sides with buildings much like it, and it looked more like a slum dwelling than a church. But it had been home to him—warm, safe, and comfortable. He suddenly loved it and missed it.

Making sure that there was no movement at all in the yard, Ian bent at the waist and walked toward the building, keeping his head down below the tops of the weeds. Mercy and Hope followed.

At the edge of the field, Ian stopped and looked once more, making sure that no one was around. As swiftly and quietly as he could, he ran toward the door he had used as his outside access. Reaching to open it, he found the knob unwilling to turn. Surely it couldn't be locked! He had been so careful to leave the door unlocked each time he went to the playground, and he had even left the door slightly ajar so he could get in and out of the building without making much noise. He pulled hard, but the door felt like it was locked tight. The cats meowed expectantly. Ian tried to think what to do. He couldn't stand there much longer. The sun would come up soon. Ian thought about the door in the alley that he had entered originally. Should he try to re-enter the building from there? Should he run? Whose hand had grabbed him? Would the person turn him in?

Run or stay/Which way? Run or stay/Which way?

Frank hated it when his father called him "boy." And Charles Benson only called his son that when he meant to condescend, which was often.

"Dad, I called Pete over in Mobile, I called Sammy over in Marianna, and a couple of long-lost fraternity brothers I could think of who lived in the Panhandle," Frank tried to explain. "They all said they'd ask around and see if their locals had heard or seen anything."

"Well, I didn't buy that police scanner to take up space in my garage, boy." Frank cringed. "Go over there and get it and use it. You can't depend on hearsay or the babblings of a bunch o' good ol' boys you knew once to get this job done. Do I need to come home and take care o' this myself?" When his father said that, Frank had flashbacks to family vacations when he and his brother, Steve, had started wrestling in the backseat of the Impala. Charles not only threatened to stop the car and take his belt to the rowdy boys, but he had done it enough times that Frank still got sick to his stomach when he had to ride in the backseat.

"No, Daddy. I'll take care of it. I'll let you know when I hear something." Frank slammed down the phone and ran his hands through his hair. He sat on the edge of his bed and looked at the clock. It was only 6:00 A.M. Charles Benson had always made sure that everybody else in the world stayed on his schedule.

The smells in the alley were familiar. Garbage, old buildings, and doughnuts. The week before, Ian had been a fugitive, a hungry, scared fugitive. Today he was a hungry, annoyed tenant who had been locked out of his place. No one seemed to be stirring in the alley, but there was definitely activity in the bakery. Mercy and Hope left Ian to go scrounge donuts from the baker, he guessed. They paced excitedly in front of the door until a man came. Ian crouched down behind the garbage cans and listened.

"Well, you two. Looks like you could use a little breakfast. Here's some day-olds and milk. How 'bout that?" said the man. Apparently, the cats made themselves at home all over the neighborhood. Ian figured that's why they looked so plump for alley cats.

While the cats were lapping at the milk, Ian crossed the alley and approached the kitchen door. The knob wouldn't budge. But Ian remembered his trick from last time. He pushed at the door and it opened just like before. Either this was a lucky coincidence or that lock needed to be fixed. He wondered if George knew about it. Once inside, Ian stopped and listened. He heard nothing in the building. Mercy and Hope had apparently gone on to scavenge elsewhere. There was no movement or sound anywhere.

The leftovers in the refrigerator were looking a little watery and wilted, but they were still edible, and Ian found his usual spoon and helped himself.

It was Monday morning, he figured. Ian wondered if Pastor Jim would come to the church. He wondered how Abbie was doing, if she was going to get out of the hospital that day. He wondered what time George would get there to clean. He thought about the lady at the keyboard and the old man who seemed to be in charge when the pastor was absent. And then Ian marveled that he knew these people, some by name, like they were family or friends, even though he'd never really met them. And he thought how they seemed to love and respect each other and how one hurt when another hurts. Ian himself hurt inside just thinking about how he had almost lost the safety of this place. Then Ian wondered again who it was who had grabbed him by the shoulder on the dark playground. Suddenly his breakfast turned sour.

Frank felt stupid looking for the scanner. What did his dad need with a three-hundred-channel scanner anyway? he wondered. Since Charles had retired, he had tried taking up some hobbies besides fishing and drinking, but he had eventually abandoned them all. That's where the golf clubs, the band saw, the tennis rackets in his garage came from. Frank waded through the junk and finally found the Bear Cat scanner next to the pneumatic drill that had only been used twice.

Jo had barely heard of quiche, much less ever tasted it. Jean assured Jo that Sue Ellen's Florentine version was the best this side of the Mississippi. Jo admitted that it tasted very good, but when Sue Ellen told her the recipe, Jo thought it was the lazy woman's way of fixing breakfast. Dump all the ingredients into a pie shell and bake it. It was almost shameful. The muffins on the side were tasty, but Jo missed her homemade biscuits and pear preserves a little. She missed her bed. She missed Ian. She hoped to satisfy Jean's need for a vacation and get back to Crestview where maybe Ian was still hiding.

Hank wasn't surprised to hear from Jo Monday morning. He had actually checked through the weekend reports first thing after he came to the station so he'd have something to tell her when she called. She sounded anxious on the phone and even more so when Hank informed her that there had not been a word about Ian's whereabouts.

"Miz Anderson, there's not been anything on Ian yet,

155

but you know that I've got your cell phone number and that I'd call you in a heartbeat should anything come in," Hank tried to encourage her.

"But I don't know if that phone will work out here or not," Jo said, trying not to sound too distraught.

"Tell you what. Why don't I call you right back on that number and you can see right then if the service out there is good?" he asked kindly.

When the phone rang, Jo jumped. She pushed the button marked "Talk." She hated to admit it, but the reception was excellent.

"I've been praying for you, Miz Anderson."

"Oh, you don't need to pray for me, Hank. Just pray that we'll find Ian," Jo spoke loudly and overenunciated each word.

Hank chuckled a bit, holding his phone receiver a little farther away from his ear. "I've been praying for him too. I promise I'll do whatever I can to find Ian."

Jo thanked God for Hank, put the cell phone in the pocket of her duster, and joined her friends on the veranda for morning coffee and a fruit plate.

Chapter Seventeen

Charles Benson mixed

another drink before the effects of the last one wore off. The more he thought about the whole Ed Lane thing, the more he wanted to escape. He thought he had resolved the matter weeks before, but the scheme hadn't worked just as he'd planned. The money that the insurance company had had to pay out was not the problem. The company could afford it. And the other people involved had been paid well to keep silent. Charles was lamenting more the fact that there was still one person who could unearth the truth, and that person was nowhere to be found.

The doctor made his rounds early, but Jim was there even earlier. He wanted to make sure that he talked to the doctor about his wife's condition.

"We don't really know what causes eclampsia, Reverend

Copeland," the young doctor explained. "We just know that the only cure for it is to deliver the baby. After that, the mother's body seems to get back to normal fairly quickly." This was information Jim had already been told, but he waited to ask when he could take Abbie home.

The doctor opened a metal folder and studied the contents for a second. "Looks like her BP, her blood pressure, is approaching normal again. Her vitals are stable and she's been up walking around. That's good. Good for circulation. I'll let the nurses check the stitches, but I don't know why you couldn't take her home today."

Jim smiled. "Really?"

"Sure. I'll write the orders right after I see her one last time. We'll need to monitor her BP closely. Sometimes the hypertension lasts after pregnancy, and she may need medication to keep it stable." The doctor looked at Jim, who looked at him with questions. "Also, there's a possibility this could happen with her next pregnancy, but there's no guarantee either way. I'd say it'd be your decision if you want to try again. We would need to put her on high-risk monitoring next time."

Jim didn't feel any sense of relief from those words. He knew how much Abbie had wanted children, and he knew she'd want to try again even weighing the risks. But he didn't want to see her repeat this agony. He couldn't get that image out of his mind of Abbie having a seizure in their own bed. The sense of panic still plagued him when he thought about it. And then there was the memory of his lifeless son lying in his arms as he and Abbie had said goodbye to him. They had both been too stunned to cry. They had simply kissed his tiny forehead and then had given him to the neonatal nurse, who had taken him away.

Jim's heart ached all over again. He had thought that it

would have gone away by now, but the grief was still fresh. But then he remembered his own sermon of the day before. He remembered the story of David. So, silently Jim worshiped God.

Thibodeaux had learned to make beignets from his grandmother, a true Cajun woman who had lived in the bayou. There was an art, she had told him, to making the French pastries.

"Don' cha know, bebe, dat der needs to be air inside dem, nuttin' else," she had said as she instructed him to cook the pastries in the right oil at the right temperature to make them light and fluffy. Thibodeaux followed her recipe exactly, right down to the fresh powdered sugar that coated them. Though he sold other pastries in his shop, the beignets were his specialty.

"Hello, Preacher," the proprietor greeted Jim as he walked into the shop. "How's Miz Abbie today?" Thibodeaux asked.

"Well, as a matter of fact, Tibby, she's right out there in the car. We're on our way home from the hospital, and she wanted me to stop in and get some beignets." Jim pointed to the street where Abbie waved from the car.

"All right. All fresh, of course, just out of the fryer." Jim's mouth watered. He loved the pastries as much as Abbie did. "On the house."

"Oh, Tibby, you don't have to do that," Jim argued.

"No, just a little something to say how sorry I am about, you know, your little one." Thibodeaux lowered his voice and looked away to avoid getting too emotional.

Jim graciously accepted the gift and walked out of the

bakery with a white bag full of warm sugary confections.

As Jim and Abbie pulled away from the curb, a city police car pulled up. Two uniformed policemen went in to talk to Tibby.

The rhymes were rolling over and over in his mind. Ian hadn't sought out this mental refuge much at all in the past week, but since the playground incident, it seemed he couldn't stop. The emptiness in the bottom of his stomach coupled with the stress of what to do next made him so nauseous that he hadn't slept all night.

The morning sun streamed through the stained glass, but it hurt Ian's eyes to look at it. He just clenched his stomach and rolled on his side, away from the glass shepherd's gaze.

Finally he slept, but he awakened to faint sounds in the basement.

Jo felt empty-handed with the other ladies carrying casserole dishes. It was usually she who organized and cooked meals for the sick or bereaved. So, even though she didn't even know the young pastor and his wife, when Jo entered the old church basement, the guilt was almost overwhelming.

"I'm sorry, Jean, that you and Jo had to tag along to this. It's just that I'd promised to bring something when Abbie came home from the hospital. Rather than us all converging over at the pastorium when Abbie doesn't need company, we thought we'd bring all our food here, and one of the younger women will take it over there for us," Sue Ellen said.

"Oh, honey, it's OK. Jo and I just wish we could do

something. We feel like we ought to," Jean answered.

Jo looked around the Broad Street Church basement. It was clean but very outdated. Jo had imagined that a city church would have been much better equipped than her own small town church kitchen. But then again, the part of the city where the building sat looked like it had seen better years.

"Oh, look at this refrigerator, would you? Looks like it hasn't been cleaned out in months. Yes, I recognize Martha's macaroni salad from our last circle meeting. My goodness," Sue Ellen fretted as she took out each bowl of leftovers, uncovered the contents, and smelled it. At most dishes she frowned or moaned and dumped the food into the large garbage can next to the pantry. Jean and Jo helped to wash the dishes in the large porcelain sink. Before most of the other ladies arrived with their food items, the refrigerator was cleaned out and the dishes were stacked neatly on the sideboard. Jo felt at least a little helpful.

Sue Ellen introduced Jo and Jean to each lady who came to bring food. Sue Ellen also gave a quick history of each one too, about her grown children or her dead husband or her recent surgeries. Jo was cordial, as was Jean, but Jo didn't really care about these people that much. Every five minutes or so, Jo would reach into her purse and look at the display on her cell phone. She was afraid that she hadn't heard it ring or that the signal was not strong enough to reach her.

Before the ladies left, they all gathered in a circle, held hands, and Sue Ellen voiced a prayer for the Copelands. Jo hoped that her phone wouldn't ring during the prayer. The thought distracted her so much that she didn't even join the prayer silently until the very end. Jo did have a concern for this pastor and his wife, but she had lost a child too. The difference was, perhaps hers was still alive somewhere.

"Amen." The women began to disperse through the basement door, reminding each other of their next circle meeting in two weeks.

"Now then," Sue Ellen said, satisfied that she had properly received, organized, and blessed the food offerings in the refrigerator. "Melanie will come by later and pick up the food and carry it over to Abbie and Brother Jim. Let's go have brunch down at one of my favorite little bistros. It's down in Daphne on our way back to Point Clear," Sue Ellen told them as they climbed into her Cadillac. Jo and Jean would agree to anything. They were on her agenda for the next few days. Backing out of the alley, Sue Ellen slammed on the brakes.

"My stars!" Sue Ellen exclaimed. "Where did he come from?" she said, looking in her rearview mirror. Jo and Jean were so startled at the abrupt stop that they didn't see anything for a moment. Finally they saw the man standing behind the car, looking as startled as the women. Jean pushed the button for the electric window on her side.

"Don't roll down your window, Jean!"

Jean quickly pushed the button again to put the window up.

"Why not? I was going to tell the man we were sorry we almost hit him," Jean explained.

"No! There are homeless people down around here all the time asking for handouts . . . or worse." Sue Ellen stepped on the gas pedal and made an exit from the alley that Jo thought Magnum P.I. would be proud of. Quickly they rode away to the safety of the suburbs.

Frank's club sandwich stuck in his throat. He took a

huge gulp of sweet tea.

"How's your daddy?" Lillian asked, filling his tea glass.

Frank swallowed hard and felt the stress of his situation follow the sandwich to the pit of his stomach.

"Fine."

His father was the last thing Frank wanted to talk about, and he hoped that Lillian would leave him alone. He knew he should have brought the scanner with him, so he wouldn't miss some late-breaking news on the boy, but he refused to carry that thing around. And besides, he didn't really care about the boy anyway. He was sure that the kid would not surface. Frank figured Ian was either dead or had run away so far that no one would ever find him. At least, that's what Frank would tell his father.

Ian wasn't sure what time it was, or even what day it was, when he awoke. He figured it was either dusk or dawn because the natural light in the building was very dim. No, he didn't know what time it was, but he knew one thing: He was not well. He had only been sick a few times in his life, most of them bad colds or something, but Ian was sure that this time it was serious. Chills wracked his body and every muscle ached. Even his eyeballs hurt. For the first time in his memory, he felt helpless, like he wanted somebody to take care of him. But he was afraid to ask for help, afraid to turn himself in. Then a thought occurred to him. Maybe this was his punishment for running. Like Jonah, he was paying a price for refusing to face his responsibilities. Ian tried to remember what Jonah had prayed before God had released him from the fish. But the words had not sunk in. As dusk turned into night, Ian slipped into a feverish sleep.

Chapter Eighteen

Hank logged on to the crime center website and then scanned the reports filed in the past twenty-four hours. There were a few new warrants issued in the Panhandle. A child molester, a murder suspect, a rapist. Even in his line of work, Hank never ceased to be amazed and repulsed by the sins of man. He sometimes wished he could just see these as faceless cases, but he often ached for the victims and their families. Then he thought of Ian, and he prayed that he would not fall into the hands of someone who would do him harm.

Hank broadened his search to include south Georgia. "A mysterious death on Lake Seminole, unidentified adult male, investigation pending autopsy results."

South Alabama. Mobile. "Suspect being held on suspicion of drug trafficking. Charges pending." This caught Hank's eye. "Suspect insists that he made contact with runaway boy."

✦ ✦ ✦

"Mr. Benson, there's somebody on line one who says his name is Pete and he wants to speak to Repeat." Marilyn rolled her eyes as she spoke into the intercom. She had heard it all, seen it all, and had learned to keep her mouth shut.

Frank grinned. "Yo dog," he said into the phone, trying to recapture the essence of their long-gone youth.

"Hey," Pete answered but without the playfulness Frank had expected.

"What's up?"

"Maybe nothing, maybe something," Pete said. "First, have you heard from your daddy lately?" he asked.

"Uh, yeah, he's up at the lake. Why?"

"No reason, just heard somebody got killed up there last night. Mysterious circumstances. Found it on the web."

"Well, I haven't talked to him today, but I was expecting to."

"Might want to give him a call just to check on him."

"OK." Frank was a little concerned.

"Another thing. This might not be anything, but we just picked up a homeless guy for questioning on a drug charge. This guy says he's encountered a runaway boy," Pete explained.

"Where?"

"Here in Mobile. He's been hanging around down at the docks and then was spotted under the interstate bridge. Some kids caught with a couple of dime bags gave us a description of a dealer that matches this guy. He's clean so far. We're running prints on him now. Don't know if the kids are telling the truth. Don't know if the guy's telling the truth. Just thought it might be something to look into."

"Anybody checking out the guy's story yet?" Frank asked.

"Uh, well, no. Not yet." Pete was trying to keep his voice down. Apparently this case was in his control, and he didn't want to let it be known he was sitting on it. "Thought I'd give you a call before I put somebody over there to look around."

"Thanks, buddy. You know I don't want any harm to come to that boy. I'd just like to find him first before they scare him away. He's a little irritable, I think." Frank tried to sound sincere.

"Yeah." Pete knew his friend's motives might not be pure, but he didn't want to know any more. He had already violated a code or two by calling Frank in the first place.

As soon as Frank hung up with Pete, Marilyn buzzed on the intercom. "Mr. Benson, your father on line two."

Jo admitted that the warm sun felt good. She laid back in the chaise longue and let the warmth bathe her face for a while. Jo had seldom indulged herself in luxuries. She and Harlan had hardly even traveled out of Okaloosa County, much less out of the state. However, when she and Harlan were newlyweds, they had gone down to Grayton Beach and taken a picnic lunch. The snow-white dunes had been so beautiful that Jo hadn't believed they were real. The sand between her toes was so warm and soft, and every footstep made a squeaking sound as they walked hand in hand along the shore. Jo hadn't thought about Harlan in a while. She had missed him so much in the beginning, and even though she had gotten used to being alone, she would forget herself and call out to him from time to time. Lately, however, she had been so focused on Ian that she hadn't thought about her late husband.

A short surge of electricity ran through her body. She had never felt that kind of sensation before. It didn't hurt, but it was troublesome, nevertheless. Again. Another short surge. Jo opened her eyes and looked around. She was totally alone on the veranda. Both Jean and Sue Ellen were napping in the house. Again the surge hit her. Standing up, she heard something fall off the chaise and onto the tile floor. The cell phone.

"Oh, my!" Jo exclaimed. She remembered she had set the phone to vibrate while her friends were sleeping. She fumbled for it. It vibrated again. She grabbed it and suddenly forgot how to answer it. Finally, after pressing all the buttons, she heard a voice.

"Miz Anderson?" Jo put the phone to her ear.

"Yes?" She tried to raise the antenna with one hand and hold onto the phone with the other, but in doing so she dropped it again. "Oh, no!"

"Miz Anderson?" Jo could still hear the voice. At least she hadn't hung up or broken the phone. Finally, with raised antenna, she took a breath.

"Yes, this is Josephine Anderson," she finally answered.

"Hey, Miz Anderson. This is Hank Thomas at the police station. I found something on the state report this morning."

After a nap, Abbie was hungry. The doctor had said that an appetite was a good sign. She found Jim sitting at his desk in the extra bedroom studying.

"Hey, honey," Jim said softly, standing to get her a chair. She sat and he kneeled down in front of her.

"Hey." Abbie had always appreciated Jim's tenderness. He was so gentle. She knew he would make a good father.

"While you were sleeping, Melanie brought over tons of food. Apparently the ladies' circle got together and has us set up with meals for the rest of the week. We've got casseroles, some frozen for later; we've got pot roast and potatoes; we've got cakes, pies, you name it. I ate a little bit of the chicken and dumplings Catherine Sizemore made," Jim said sheepishly. "Let me heat up something for you."

"I am a little hungry. Do we have any more beignets?"

Thibodeaux had seen the man in the picture. In fact, he had given him day-olds that he had planned to throw out. Of course, Tibby had given some to the other alley cats that wandered the streets too. The policemen just wanted to know if he'd seen the man do anything suspicious, like meeting kids in the alley. Thibodeaux knew what a drug deal looked like. He had seen it happen lots of times, but before he had been able to get police down to where he had seen it, the dealers and the buyers had been long gone. No, the suspect the police were asking about wasn't one of the ones he'd seen pushing drugs. He just looked like another down-on-his-luck bum.

Ian was glad that he had saved some grape juice and crackers. Even though he wasn't hungry—in fact, he was nauseous—he knew he needed to keep up his strength. He didn't even want to think about the peanut butter. The first serving of juice and crackers stayed down. Ian even felt a little better, just a little. He ate another cracker and another half cup of juice. His headache was subsiding a bit. He thought that maybe he had just been weak from hunger and not really sick at all. By the third serving, he realized he was wrong. When hot saliva started collecting in his mouth, he knew it was time to get to the bathroom quickly. He got there just in time.

By the time Frank got to the police station, the suspect had been released. After a few expletives under his breath, Frank set up a time to meet with Pete after-hours, and then he got a room at the Mobile Marriott and waited for Pete to call.

"Why'd you let him go, man?" Frank asked his friend when he finally called.

"Had to. Couldn't pin anything on him, except public drunkenness. After he sobered up, we had to release him. It's the law," Pete tried to explain.

"Since when did that matter to you?" Frank had never talked to his old buddy like that before.

"Since I became a police officer, Frank!" Pete hadn't called Frank by his real name in years. Even though Frank was annoyed at Pete, he didn't want to offend him. He would need information gathered during the interrogation to find Ian.

Frank apologized and Pete calmed down.

"OK, where exactly did the old guy say he saw the boy?" Frank asked.

"We couldn't ever really get that out of him. He was pretty soused when we picked him up. However, I can sort of give you a general area."

"Thanks, man. I appreciate it."

Jo told Jean and Sue Ellen the news.

"Wouldn't that be a coincidence if the boy was Ian?" Sue Ellen said.

"Well, speaking of coincidences, what if that man we almost ran over yesterday morning was the guy in question?" Jean added. "It'd be almost spooky, you know."

"Spooky or not, I've got to check this out either way. I can't go home until I'm sure Ian's not here."

"How could he have gotten all the way over here?" Jean asked.

"Could have hopped a train, hitched a ride on a truck. You don't know Ian," Jo said, realizing that she really didn't know Ian either.

"I know this city like the back of my hand, honey. We'll just go on a fact-finding mission of our own first thing in the morning," Sue Ellen said, serving her guests a dinner of jambalaya and flat corn bread.

"See, I told you coming to Mobile was a good idea," Jean gloated.

Chapter Nineteen

This is a good place

to start, girls," Sue Ellen drawled as she pulled the Cadillac into the bakery parking space.

"Smells really good," Jo said from the backseat. "What's their specialty?"

"Beignets," Sue Ellen answered.

"What?" Jean asked.

"It's like a French doughnut. It's so good. You can get 'em down in New Orleans in the French Quarter. Y'all ever been to Café DuMonde? Well, Tibby is Cajun, and he learned how to make the pastries like those people down there. My stars, they're the best."

Jo and Jean didn't argue. Sounded like Sue Ellen and Tibby knew what they were doing.

✦ ✦ ✦

Jim still felt stuffed from the eating he had done the

night before. He fixed Abbie a bagel with cream cheese and a large orange juice, but he didn't feel hungry at all. The chicken and dumplings, the butter beans, the broccoli casserole, the coconut pie he had eaten were still "sticking to his ribs."

"Melanie said she would come over later this morning to stay with me," Abbie said, finishing her bagel.

"Oh?" Jim responded. "But your mother is still here."

"I know, but Melanie wants to lend a hand. I thought you'd probably like to get down to the church for a while today, and I don't want you to worry," Abbie said.

"Well, yeah, I guess I could do that if you're sure Melanie doesn't mind."

Jim couldn't believe all that had happened in his life in the past week. Just a few days before, Abbie had had a seizure, an emergency C-section, and a baby boy who died and was buried. He had run the gamut of emotions. Fear, anger, grief, despair. Yet more and more he could see God at work.

Melanie and her husband, Dan, knew what Jim and Abbie were going through. Though they had two young children, she had lost their first one just like Abbie had. Melanie was the first person Jim remembered to call after they brought Abbie in. Leaving the children with Dan, she had made her way to the hospital as soon as she could. And Melanie had talked Abbie through the day-to-day struggles she was having with pain and grief. Dan did his part by watching the kids while his wife ministered to Abbie as no one else could.

As he pulled into his parking space next to the church, Jim noticed Sue Ellen's big yellow Cadillac parked in front of Tibby's bakery. He wondered why Sue Ellen was in town on a Wednesday morning. He had heard she was already moved in to her new house in Point Clear. Jim loved Sue Ellen, one of several wealthy widows in his congregation. She was generous with her money and time and was a true Southern lady, complete with the drawl. When her husband died, Jim was afraid he'd lose Sue Ellen from his congregation. She had wanted to move out of her home in town and scale down to a smaller, newer place. So when she did move out, Jim was afraid she wouldn't want to drive back to town to worship. However, so far Sue Ellen had made the drive willingly.

"Why, Preacher, what are you doing here?" Sue Ellen cooed as Jim came up behind her and patted her on the shoulder.

"Saw your car over here, Miss Sue Ellen," Jim said. "Couldn't resist Tibby's beignets, huh?"

Sue Ellen introduced the ladies. "Preacher, I'd like you to meet two of my friends from over in Crestview. This is Emma Jean Mayer, a sorority sister of mine from Montevallo days. And this is her friend Josephine Anderson."

"Ladies." The young pastor greeted them. "What brings you downtown this morning?" Jim asked.

"Well . . ." Sue Ellen looked at Jo to see if it was all right to tell the story to her pastor. After a pause, Jo nodded. Sue Ellen invited Jim to sit down at their table, and the ladies told Brother Copeland the whole story.

"So, you see, we thought we'd come down here ourselves and look around. As soon as Tibby gets through with the breakfast rush, we've got some questions to ask him."

"Well, any friend of Miss Sue Ellen's is a friend of mine," Tibby said with a slight Cajun accent after he was introduced to Jean and Jo. "Beignet on the house?"

Jo still didn't know what a beignet was, but then again

175

she had been introduced to several tasty new dishes on this trip. The sweet pastry melted in her mouth. She was sure that she had powdered sugar all over her face, but she didn't really care. A big gulp of cold milk washed down the sweet concoction. She was so mesmerized by the taste that Jo almost forgot why she and the other ladies had come into the bakery.

"Oh, yeah," Tibby said, sitting down at the table with the ladies and Jim. "De police come first asking about de homeless man dat hangs around here sometime. T'ink the smell of fresh-baked goods bring him in. Never have no money. Just hang around. I give him day-olds sometime. I tell the police all I know." Jo thought that Tibby's slight accent was intriguing.

"Did the man ever say anything about seeing a little boy around here, Mr. Thibodeaux?" Jo was curious.

"Just call me Tibby, ma'am. No, never talk to de man really. He just hungry and I feed," Tibby continued. "Somet'ing else I can get you ladies? Pastor?"

They all looked at each other and realized that they didn't need but really wanted another pastry.

Tibby smiled. "I bring more beignets."

Ian's shirt was soaked. Apparently he had sweated in his sleep. But at least he felt a little better. He had kept his body pretty clean so far in his daily spa excursions, but until then he had not felt the need for laundry services. However, with the shirt stuck to him, he was aware of its odor, and he knew he had to wash a few things out. He had seen some robes and towels in the room with the big galoshes. He would at least have something to put on while his clothes dried.

He could tell he was still weak. It took all his strength to wring out his shirt and jeans.

The water felt soothing to his nude body. He could almost feel the sickness leave him as he floated.

As he crossed the alley to the church, Jim thought about the whole story of the missing boy and the homeless man. He had seen lots of homeless men hanging around or sleeping under the nearby interstate, but he had not encountered many of them. However, there had been one who had come early a couple of Saturday mornings before asking for food. Jim had given him some pocket change, and he had encouraged the man to spend it on food and not on liquor. Then Jim wondered if the man had complied. He wondered too if the boy allegedly sighted was the same boy whose picture had been on the flyer, the one he had angrily crumpled up, the one later distributed by the policeman who had been sitting in his church service. That would be so many coincidences that he couldn't believe it. As he grabbed the knob to unlock the basement door, he was surprised that the door came open fairly easily with a slight push. Jim wondered how long the door had been that way. It would have to be fixed, he thought, before the day was out. Though the church had never been burglarized, the neighborhood was a high-crime area. Even Tibby had had bars put on his windows and doors.

Jim marveled at how clean the refrigerator looked inside. Then he remembered Sue Ellen saying that she'd cleaned it out the day before. He noticed the various casserole dishes and plastic containers sitting on the sideboard. He'd have to remember to make an announcement at the beginning of prayer meeting reminding ladies to pick up their dishes in the kitchen. He placed the plastic grocery bag of food Abbie had insisted he take in the almost-empty refrigerator. The bag was full. That would be more than enough for his lunch that day.

Ian was pretty sure that it was afternoon. George had come in to vacuum the auditorium and dust the big tables at the front. Also, the sun was coming in through the stained-glass window at the right angle. Ian could tell by how it illuminated the shepherd mosaic that it was mid-afternoon. The sickness had interrupted Ian's mental calendar, however, and he couldn't tell if it was Tuesday or Wednesday afternoon. It didn't matter, really. It was just that he wanted to be aware of every detail that affected him. It might be necessary for survival.

Even though the phone woke him out of a drunken sleep, Charles Benson welcomed the news. Frank was sure that his father would be happy to know that he had somewhat of a lead. Even though his search had led him absolutely nowhere, Frank reported, by hugely embellishing the facts, that he was practically breathing down the boy's neck.

Charles fixed another Slammer to celebrate and realized he was getting low on gin. That was a critical issue he'd have to remedy. He'd call his driver to pick some up on his way out to the lake.

"You did good, boy," the elder Benson said good-naturedly.

"Uh, yeah, thanks, Dad. So when are you coming home from the lake?"

"Well, I was going home later today, but since you've got everything under control, I might just stay here the rest of the week. There's nothing to go home to," Charles said. Frank detected a lot of sadness in his father's voice. Ever since Frank's mother died the year before, his father had slipped in and out of depression. Charles's alcohol consumption had increased gradually to the point where Frank worried about his father, even more than usual. Frank had pleaded with Charles to quit driving the boat just as he had quit driving the car, but Charles wouldn't hear of it. Frank wondered what would get him first—the alcohol or the lake.

Ian's stomach was still a little tentative, so he tried the crackers and juice in small doses. He decided to stop at two helpings, the second with a small amount of peanut butter. Satisfied that they would stay down, he lay down on his mattress and read through the books again. He liked the stories he read and reread, even though they were beneath his reading level. Ian liked the pictures too. The Man, Jesus, seen in almost all the pictures, apparently had been a great Man. He had healed the sick and raised the dead and had loved children. Though he wasn't sure how it all fit together, Ian was beginning to realize that God had sent Jesus from heaven. He wasn't sure why or how or even when this had all happened, but he was starting to feel sad and happy at the same time when he thought about God. It was a funny feeling he had inside, or was that the crackers and juice trying to tell him something?

The ladies were exhausted. Hank had called in the afternoon to give them the name on the police report: Jeremiah Mock. After they had talked to Tibby, getting from him a description of the homeless man, then getting the name from Hank, the ladies had ridden practically all over Mobile looking for him. They had stopped by Sue Ellen's son's law office and had asked him and his partners to keep their eyes open for information on the homeless man and the boy. Mock had been listed as a transient, no address of any kind, but no criminal record either. Knowing his name hadn't helped them at all. The ladies had asked around using his name, at homeless shelters, at the marina, at secondhand clothing shops, at the bus and train stations—everywhere they could think of that a homeless man might go. They even stopped people on the street and asked if they knew him. It was as if the man had vanished. Maybe he had been spooked by the police interrogation and had moved on to another city. Either way, the trail was cold.

Frank arrived at the bakery during the afternoon lull.

"Yeah, his aunt sure is concerned about de boy," Tibby said.

"What?" Frank stopped in mid-bite.

Though Thibodeaux had never met anyone he didn't like, the man standing in front of him feeding his face with a chocolate doughnut made Tibby a little nervous for some reason.

"You mean she's here?" Frank laid the doughnut down and wiped his hands on a napkin.

"Uh, yeah," Tibby said tentatively. "But I tell her what I tell you. I know dat homeless man who hangs around here sometimes, but he say nothing 'bout a small boy. So, dat be all, mister . . . uh," Tibby said, writing a receipt for a doughnut and coffee.

"I'm just a friend of the family, somebody who cares about the boy, too, but I didn't know Miz Anderson had come over here. Maybe we could have come together," Frank said, paying his bill.

"Oh, she come with her friend, Jean something-or-other, and dey stay with Miss Sue Ellen at Point Clear."

"Point Clear?"

"Yeah, down farther on de bay," Tibby answered.

"Think they're there now?" Frank was trying to sound nonchalant.

"No, dey'll probably be in town today and stay for preaching at church. That's what Miss Sue Ellen would do," Tibby said.

Ian thought that he looked a little like Jesus in the pictures. His own clothes were still drying, so he didn't have a choice but to wear a white robe. Ian pretended in his mind that he was the Man going about doing good. He wondered what it was like to love and be loved by so many people.

Voices started as distant mumbles, but then the auditorium doors opened and people started coming in. He didn't know what they were there for. It wasn't Sunday morning already, was it? No, it was night, sometime in the middle of the week. He quietly slipped out of the room and sat in the hallway, wondering if there would be music. There was, and Ian waited until it had passed.

His appetite was starting to come back, he noticed. In fact, he was downright hungry. He hoped that the refrigerator would be well stocked. He planned to make a late-night trip to find out.

The music stopped and Ian could barely hear the pastor's voice. Ian started to crawl back into his room and watch and listen to the man speak, but he decided to stay in the hallway instead. It was a change of pace, at least.

Jo and Jean both went to sleep on the way back to Point Clear. Sue Ellen had had to open the car window and let the wind hit her in the face to stay awake. She knew this wasn't good for her hairdo, but she would rather go to the beauty parlor than the funeral parlor, she thought. Sue Ellen giggled at her own joke.

As they drove into the driveway, the ladies were so weary that they did not notice the car that followed them.

Chapter Twenty

It was the wee hours, and Ian felt safe in rummaging through the kitchen. He was shocked to find the refrigerator so bare. Except for the plastic sack on the top rack, there was nothing much. His mouth watered. What he wouldn't give for casserole leftovers! He wondered what was in the sack. It won't hurt to look, he thought. Ah, yes, plastic containers stacked with meat loaf, roast beef, fruit salad, and cake! But why had they been put together in a sack? Maybe that had been a part of the tidiness plan, to keep all the foods together in one bag. It didn't matter why; Ian just knew that this might save his life.

As he ate, careful not to eat too fast, he noticed the tools sitting by the basement door. A close inspection revealed that someone, probably George, had fixed the lock on the back door. Ian would have to make sure that he didn't lock himself out again when he went out to the playground—that is, if he got up the nerve to go back to the playground again.

When Abbie reminded him to take leftovers for lunch, Jim remembered that he hadn't eaten the ones he had taken the day before.

"I got busy answering mail and working on my sermon, and then I had to run out to make a visit at the hospital, so I forgot about the food in the fridge. I just grabbed a burger on my way back to the church. I'll try to remember today."

"Melanie's coming over around ten, as soon as she gets the kids to her mother's," Abbie said.

"Great! Oh, that reminds me. Hunter made a profession of faith last night."

"He did?" Abbie had been asleep when Jim came in from prayer meeting. Abbie was glad to hear the news. She had had the eight-year-old in her Sunday school class. She had shared the plan of salvation with him a few weeks before. He had prayed the sweetest prayer.

"Yep. We're gonna have a baptism this Sunday. My first since coming here," Jim said happily before kissing his wife good-bye.

Jo hardly recognized Hank wearing regular clothes instead of his police uniform. And she was shocked to see him standing on Sue Ellen's front porch, especially so early in the morning.

"What are you doing here, Hank?" Jo asked.

"Miz Anderson, I got some information that really concerned me, so I thought I'd take a vacation day and come over here and tell you myself."

Jo was alarmed. "Well, I'd about decided to go on home

today. Ian's not here."

"I wouldn't be too sure, Miz Anderson, and I'm even more concerned about his safety now," Hank continued.

"Why?"

"There was a murder a couple of days ago over on Lake Seminole," Hank said.

"Uh-huh."

"The man was identified as Steven Powell from Madison. His nickname was 'Trooper.'"

The name didn't ring a bell with Jo.

"This man was Ed Lane's good friend. He and another guy named Nicholas Register were drinking buddies with Ed."

Jo still wasn't sure what all this had to do with Ian.

Hank continued. "Powell died of multiple stab wounds to the back."

"Oh, how awful," Jo interjected.

"And just a week ago, Nicholas—they called him Nick—was found dead of an apparent suicide."

"That's terrible," Jo said, but then a light came on in her memory. "Nick and Trooper. Those two gentlemen were at Mary and Ed's funeral. The only ones there except the pastor, his wife, Ian, and me. What does this all mean, Hank?"

"It means something for sure, Miz Anderson. I also found out that Frank Benson is here in Mobile doing the same thing you are."

"Here? Is he looking for the homeless man . . . but how did he know?" Jo asked.

"No telling. He could have a friend on the force over here or something. Maybe it was a hunch. Maybe he knows even more than we do. I just know he's here. He stayed at the Marriott last night." Hank looked concerned.

"Do you think . . . nah." Jo paused to think. "Do you

185

think that Ed and Mary were being paid off by old man Benson, and maybe Nick and Trooper knew about it?" Jo was trying to decipher the news.

Hank nodded. "Not only do I think so, but maybe Nick and Trooper were even in on the arson of the house," he added.

"It was ruled accidental, Hank. What makes you think otherwise?"

"Those two guys were not on their usual barstools at their usual time the night the house burned down. They did appear later on, so the bartender said, smelling of gasoline." Hank's eyes were dancing with frightened excitement.

"The fire marshal's report . . ."

"Could have been falsified. Benson knows a lot of guys in high places. Nick and Trooper were easy to kill, and they were both known to run in rough crowds. I doubt if either death will be investigated much further. At least, they won't be a high priority."

"But why kill Ed and Mary? He was paying them well to keep quiet," Jo asked.

"I don't know. Maybe Ed was tired of the arrangement and was threatening to tell the story. Who knows? But if Ian knew the setup, maybe he was supposed to die in that fire too."

Jo covered her mouth, hoping to stop a horrified gasp. "Oh no! Ian is in danger, Hank. We have to find him."

"I think you're right. I'm out of my jurisdiction, and I don't have any real evidence to back up my theory, but I thought I'd come and help get Ian to safety before Frank Benson finds him. Then maybe we can get an investigation going."

Jo threw her arms around Hank's waist. She sobbed and thanked him.

"Found 'im!" Pete said as Frank picked up the phone in his hotel room.

"Who? Found who?" Frank asked.

"Mock, the homeless guy," Pete answered. "I've got an officer detaining him under the Fillingim Street Pedestrian Bridge."

"Where's that?"

"I'll come over and take you there myself."

Jo felt like a criminal, watching the police car pull out of the hotel parking lot with Frank Benson in it.

"I figured he had a connection on the force over here," Hank said, pulling his car out into traffic a few cars behind. "Where's he going?" Hank was talking to himself.

"I feel funny doing this, Hank," Jo said nervously.

"I understand, but since I'm out of my jurisdiction, we'll have to rely on his information to lead us to Ian."

"I know, but I feel seedy scrunching down like this in a car," Jo said, slumping so that just the top of her head could be seen over Hank's dashboard.

"Oh, think of it as a Magnum P.I. episode. That's all it is."

The two men drove slowly under the bridge where a few homeless guys were sitting. Another police car was parked nearby, and a uniformed officer was standing talking to the men.

"Drive down to the end of the block, Pete, and then turn around," Frank told his friend.

Doubling back, Pete pulled the car over to the side of the road and stopped.

"There's our man," Pete said, getting out of the car. "Looks just like his mug shot."

"What's happening, Hank? What do you see?" Jo said, trying to stay out of sight.

"Well, Frank and the cop are getting out of the car. There's already a cop out there talking to the guys. I'm gonna pull over here and try to look nonchalant."

"Oh, great." Jo was getting a twitch in her back from the slump.

"OK. That must be Mock."

"What? Where?" Jo tried to look.

"Stay down." Hank put his hand on Jo's head.

"Ian's not with him, is he? I mean, with the homeless guy. Mock."

"No. There are a couple of other old guys around. I'm gonna make one pass under the bridge so they don't spot me sitting here out in the open."

"Be careful."

"Stay down," Hank said, reaching into his glove compartment for a map.

"What are you doing?" Jo asked.

"Looking like I'm lost."

"Oh, no."

188

"It's nothing, man. We're not here to arrest you again or anything," Pete said to Mock after inviting the other men to walk away. "We just want to know more about that kid you said you saw."

Mock mumbled something.

"Ah, he's drunk, Pete," Frank said.

"No, I ain't," Mock looked up at Pete. "You cain't throw me in the tank again. I ain't drunk."

Pete leaned into Frank and whispered. "Let me handle this, OK?"

Mock lit a cigarette with trembling hands.

Jim was glad to see that George had fixed the basement door lock. Mercy and Hope scampered past as the pastor entered the building.

"Well, well, haven't seen you girls in a while. You don't look like you've starved any." Jim reached down and rubbed both of their arched backs as they purred and meowed. "Want something for breakfast?" Jim looked at his watch. "It'd be more like brunch, I guess."

While he poured the dry cat food into a dish, Jim thought about Hunter, the little boy he would baptize on Sunday. He thought about the lost boy, Ian Lane too, and he prayed for both boys, the lost one and the saved one.

"How 'bout a little milk to wash it down?" Jim said to the cats as he opened the refrigerator. Seeing the plastic sack, he salivated, thinking of the good food that would be his warmed-over lunch. He looked at his watch again and said, "Hey, maybe I need a little brunch too, guys."

Ian turned over on his mattress and opened his eyes. He had decided not to venture out into the playground the night before, but he had lain awake most of the night trying to figure out who it was he had encountered out there before. That experience had triggered dreams again about the fire. *What had really happened?* he wondered. Could he have left the stove on? Could the fire have started in the laundry room, the dryer, maybe? Ian had learned all about the laundry, about what not to wash with whites. He wore the pink T-shirt under a sweater a few times, but he never let anybody see it. The pink socks he just couldn't bring himself to wear at all.

Ian lay on his back and tried to force his memory to reveal the details of that night. He had come home from school, done his homework, heated a can of ravioli, and left what he hadn't eaten on the counter next to the stove. Or had he left it on the stove? Maybe with the eye still on? He was pretty sure he had turned off the stove. He remembered too that the clothes dryer had shut off long before he went to bed. He had folded the clothes himself and laid them on the ironing board. Had the wiring in the house been bad? It was a fairly new house. His parents hadn't smoked, so cigarettes did not cause the fire.

Suddenly he missed his parents, not so much the way they had become, but having parents at all. It was hard to remember the good times like when his mother smiled some and played with him. His father often would watch them from his bed. Sometimes Ed would smile, and Ian would think that he wanted to play with them too. But his father never joined them. He slept a lot, his mother said, from the medicines he took. The alcohol, later, made his father angry when he was awake. It made his mother sad most of the time. The good memories faded, and Ian got up the courage to let himself think again about the night of the fire.

Jim thought he remembered that he had put two pieces of cake among the leftovers. He laughed at himself. *I must be getting old,* he thought. He patted his stomach and said out loud, "And I need to work out." After his snack, he planned to go and check out the baptistery, the robes, and the waders, just to be sure everything was ready for the Sunday baptism.

The phone in the office rang, and Jim crammed the last morsel of cake into his mouth and hurried to answer.

"Hello?" Jim tried to swallow and wished he had washed down his cake with some milk.

"Pastor? Is that you?" Sue Ellen asked.

"Yes. It's me," Jim looked around the office for anything wet to drink. Yesterday's diet soda was probably flat, but he gulped it anyway just to clear his throat.

"It's Sue Ellen, Pastor. Thought I'd tell you the latest on Josephine and the lost boy."

Hank found the perfect place to hide. Pulling into a vacant space at a used car lot down the street from the bridge, he and Jo watched and waited until Frank and the two policemen finished talking to Mock. Finally, Frank and Pete got into their car and headed north. The other officer headed south, passing the car lot.

"The other cop is probably going back to the station. Let's follow Frank and see where he takes us," Hank said. Jo peeked out over the dashboard and caught a glimpse of the cruiser.

"Where do you think they're going?" she asked.

"I don't know. Maybe the guy remembered where he saw the boy, and these guys are going to check it out," Hank answered.

"Why don't we ask Mock ourselves?" Jo wanted to know.

"We could, but Frank maybe already has a head start on us, and I'd hate to let him beat us to Ian."

"Yeah, I see what you're saying." Jo prayed silently, *Lord, let us find Ian before Frank does.*

Hank was trying to establish a pattern. The two men he was following drove first to a city park. After they walked around among the playground equipment, they went from house to house in the area showing Ian's picture to whoever would come to the door.

Next the men drove to an elementary school. Looking around the building that apparently had been locked for the summer, they walked the perimeter of the playground, looking in weeds and brush along the way.

A playground. Hank wanted to see one more site before he made a final conclusion.

Finally, Frank and the officer drove to a day care center where children were playing in a fenced-in area. The two men talked for a while with a worker, showing her Ian's picture. The worker shook her head. Apparently, Mock had told the men that he had spotted Ian on a playground, but the man hadn't remembered exactly where he was in the city. The men went inside the center.

"Miz Anderson?" Hank said.

"Yes?" Jo was almost too cramped to answer. She sat up briefly and flexed her neck.

"Seems like there's a playground involved. While the guys are inside this place we need to make ourselves scarce. I don't want them to figure out they're being followed."

"What next, then?"

"Now I think it's time for us to visit Mr. Mock," Hank said, driving toward the bridge.

Thoughts of Ian and Hunter made Jim's heart heavy. He sighed at the feeling. He knew it would take some time, but it didn't take much for Jim to grieve again.

Walking up the stairs, Jim unlocked the front doors and walked down the steps and out into the yard beside the building. There was shade on the little grave, and Jim walked slowly to it. First, he plucked the dead flowers off the sprays; then he stooped down beside the fresh mound of dirt. He had ordered the headstone with James' full name, his birth and death dates that were only days apart, and the Scripture verse that he and Abbie had chosen: 1 Corinthians 15:57— "Thanks be to God, which giveth us the victory through our Lord Jesus Christ." They had always claimed victory in Christ, and He had always given them strength and courage. However, Jim knew that this victory might be slow in coming. Then he wept and, like David, worshiped God.

Rising to his feet, Jim realized that Abbie had not even seen her son's grave. He thought, however, that it might be better to wait until the headstone was in place. It would look less fresh, he thought.

A chain holding a swing squeaked when the wind blew. Jim looked up and noticed a rain cloud forming overhead. Passing the little playground, he saw a cigarette butt lying on the ground inside the fence. Opening the gate, Jim went in to retrieve the trash when he noticed an empty liquor bottle lying in some short weeds up against the fence.

"Ah, George," Jim said, making a mental note to remind the janitor to pay attention to the outside of the church as well as the inside.

Jim stepped back inside the front doors of the church just as the rain began.

By the time Hank and Jo got back to the bridge, the band of homeless men was gone. Jo had thought that these men would have sought shelter there during the rain, but as far as they could tell, their only link to Ian, Jeremiah Mock, had disappeared.

"Let's get some lunch, Miz Anderson."

"But . . . OK. I need to call Sue Ellen and Jean and give them an update," Jo answered wearily.

Jo wasn't much on fast food. In fact, she wished she had some of the casseroles that her friends back home had made for her. As she ate a cold French fry, she dialed Sue Ellen's number.

"Hey, honey, we were just thinking about you. You all right?" Sue Ellen asked.

"I'm fine. We've been playing Magnum P.I. this morning," Jo said as she tried to sound upbeat.

"Have y'all got any more information?"

"We think so. We followed Frank and this police officer around. They found Mock, the homeless guy. After they talked to him, they started looking around playgrounds in the area," Jo told her friend.

Hank motioned to Jo. "What?" Jo said to Hank. "Hang on, Sue Ellen." Jo covered the phone with her hand.

"Maybe it's best if we keep our information to ourselves," Hank told her. "Don't want too much to get out.

Certainly don't want Frank to know we're here and looking for the same thing he is."

Jo nodded. "That's all we know right now. Hey, let me speak to Jean."

Jo told Jean to go back to Crestview anytime she wanted to. Then Jo vowed to tell whomever would listen that she didn't intend to stop looking until she found Ian safe and sound.

"Miz Anderson!" Hank shouted. Jo almost dropped her cell phone. "There's Mock!"

"I'll have to call you back, Jean."

It was too much of a coincidence, Jo thought, but this man did look like the man Sue Ellen had almost run over in the alley. If Hank hadn't been there, Jo would have been scared to death to ask the man to sit in the backseat of the car.

"Hey, man, get out of the rain. You're soaked," Hank said to the man.

The stench was indescribable. The odors weren't easy to distinguish either. They were a combination of body odor, alcohol, and old food. Jo tried to politely pinch her nostrils shut.

"Hey, buddy, when was the last time you had a good meal?" Hank asked.

"I don't know," the man mumbled.

"My friend and I just had a hamburger down the street. Could we treat you to one?" Hank asked with a smile.

"Yeah."

"That's every playground, park, school in the city. Now there's also places out in the suburbs, but I can't imagine

Mock being out there," Pete said.

"Well, the old guy might not have even seen the boy on a playground. He was probably hallucinating anyway," Frank said wearily.

"I've gotta get back to the station pretty soon," Pete said. "Maybe we can start again tomorrow."

"Let me off at the hotel," Frank said dejectedly. "I want to find that kid and return him safely to his guardian."

"Tell you what, I'll check the database when I get back. I promise I'll call you if there's anything anywhere. Keep your cell nearby," Pete said as Frank got out of the car.

"Thanks, man."

As soon as Pete's cruiser was out of sight, Frank called the valet for his car. At least he could keep an eye on the yellow Cadillac. He thought maybe the old ladies knew something he didn't.

Ian sat paralyzed with fear. He drew his arms and legs to his chest, making himself a tight ball. He tried to think what to say when the person on the other side of the door found him.

Jim was a little annoyed to find so much junk on the steps and in the hallway to the baptistery. He couldn't really blame George, though. Since the church hadn't baptized anyone in a while, it's no wonder this place had been used for storage. However, he was shocked and upset to find that the roof had leaked. Water puddled in several places along the hallway and into the dressing room. Jim sighed, looking up at the ceiling to see if he could locate the exact place where the water was running in.

"Good thing I came up here today when it had rained. No telling how long before we would have found the problem," Jim said to himself. He knew there was little or no money in the building and grounds fund. The deacons had voted to fix the front steps of the church where time and wear had made them crack and buckle. The church had also added a wheelchair ramp. The older members of the congregation had had enough trouble getting around sometimes, and safe access for them had been a must. He'd have to call an emergency meeting of the deacon board on Sunday.

The robing rooms were small, but with Broad Street's static membership, the need for more space for baptismal candidates wasn't necessary. Jim checked the waders hanging in the corner to make sure they were in good shape. He couldn't chance springing a leak in them. Jim chuckled a little but admitted to himself that having his waders fill up with water would be quite embarrassing. He made a mental note to himself to bring along another set of clothes, just in case.

Jim noticed that the one small robe in the men's dressing room was missing. He had checked the baptismal robe inventory when he first came to Broad Street. Maybe he had been wrong. Maybe there had never been a small robe in that room. He was, however, pretty sure that the towel supply was lower than he remembered.

"George," he muttered to himself, thinking that perhaps George was somehow responsible for this disappearance. "Guess we can't be too hard on him. With what we pay him . . ." Jim didn't finish the sentence.

At least Ian knew who was on the other side. He recognized the pastor's voice.

Pastor, Pastor/Move on faster. He buried his head in his hands and prayed again. *Where can I go?* he said silently. Ian liked the prayer better than the rhyme. For some reason it made him not as frightened.

"I ain't done nothin' wrong. Just drinkin'. Ain't no law 'gainst that, is there?" Mock said as he crammed his mouth full. Jo looked away, hoping she wouldn't get sick looking at the food hanging out of the filthy man's mouth.

"I know. We're not here about your drinking. We want to ask you about the boy you said you saw," Hank said, handing the man a napkin that he promptly rejected.

"Done told them cops what I saw."

"You told them that you saw him in a playground, right?" Jo asked.

The man nodded.

"Is there anything else you remember about that night?" Hank continued.

"Weren't just one night I seen 'im."

"You saw him more than one night?" Hank asked.

"Was he about ten years old, blond hair, blue eyes, had on new Nike tennis shoes?" Jo lit up.

The old man nodded. "More drink!"

Hank went to the counter to refill the man's cup.

"Do you remember which playground it was where you saw him?" Hank asked, returning with a full cup of soda.

The man shrugged. "I'm all over. Gotta keep movin' to

keep the cops off my tail."

"Was it at a school?" Hank probed.

"Done told the cops I don't 'member where it was 'xactly."

Jo had never seen a man eat so much and so fast. She almost wished she could cook for him on a regular basis.

"You got a favorite liquor store, Mr. Mock?" Hank waved a ten-dollar bill in front of Mock's face.

"Hank!" Jo chided.

Mock looked at Hank and then at Jo. "You don't care 'bout me. Nobody does. That's why I'm like I am. You just don't care." Mock wadded up the hamburger wrapper and threw it on the floor.

"We're sorry, Mr. Mock," Jo said. "We do care, but right now we're looking for a little boy who's all alone, and he's in danger. Some other people are looking for him too, who might want to hurt him."

Mock sucked on the straw and did not look at his new benefactors. He did not seem convinced of their concern.

"I told Mama last week I wouldn't drink no more. Broke my promise," Jeremiah Mock finally said.

"I'm sure she loves you anyway, no matter what you do," Jo tried to sympathize, and then she was sorry she had even gotten involved with this sad man.

Mock scoffed. "What do you know?"

Hank was getting a little impatient with the man's surly attitude. "Miz Anderson here was trying to be nice. There are programs you can get in to help you stop drinking. Your mother, I'm sure, could help you find a group locally."

Mock put down the soda and looked down. "Mama's dead. Been dead ten years."

"I'm sorry. We didn't know." Jo almost reached out to touch the man.

"Thought you said you talked to your mother last week," Hank added.

"I talk to her at her grave," Mock said sadly.

"A grave? A graveyard? Is it near this playground where you saw the boy?" Hank asked.

Jo's eyes lit up.

The man nodded.

"Why didn't you tell us, Mr. Mock?" Jo asked.

"Didn't think of it till now."

"Where is the graveyard, Mr. Mock?" Hank spoke loudly, enunciating every word.

The man was silent. Jo's heart began to pound.

Finally, the man said, "Don't 'member."

Ian held his breath, literally, until the pastor's footsteps had faded completely. His stomach was tight and he felt nauseated. He wasn't sure how much longer he could seek asylum in this place. His first thought was to drain the spa when he was sure no one would hear the slurping sound of the drain. At least it was one way to cover his tracks.

The city had no records of a woman with the name Bonnie Mock having been buried in any public cemetery in the past ten years. However, her death certificate was on file. Her son had been right about the time that had passed. It had been almost ten years to the day.

"She must have been buried in a private cemetery somewhere," Hank said. "Let's get us a map of this town and see what we can find out, huh?"

Jo was so glad to have Hank there with her and so thankful that he wasn't giving up on the case. And at that moment, she did feel a little like Magnum P.I.

Chapter Twenty-One

Jim watched Abbie sleep.

He counted her breaths, and he cherished every one she took. When the phone rang, he reached for it quickly, hoping that it wouldn't wake her.

"Sorry, Pastor. I'm just now getting back to answering my messages from yesterday. Hope I didn't wake you up calling so early," Deacon Spivey said.

"No, it's OK." Jim glanced over at Abbie, who had only stirred lightly but not awakened.

"So you found a leak in the roof, huh?"

"Tell you what, let me call you right back in the other room," Jim tried to whisper before he hung up the phone, grabbed his robe and slippers, and headed for the kitchen.

"Lieutenant, here are those reports you wanted from Tallahassee. They just faxed them over," the secretary said, dropping a manila folder on Pete's desk.

Pete had lots of other higher-profile cases than the Ian Lane case, but there was something about Frank Benson's interest in the whole thing that made Pete a little uneasy. It was especially Frank's concern for the young boy's safety that didn't ring true with Pete.

Pete had never known his old buddy Frank to be the least bit compassionate. In fact, every girl who had ever dated Frank in college had found him to be arrogant and boorish. Frank's good looks, money, and flashiness had attracted the women initially; but once they got to know him, they had seen what a cad he was. Of course, Pete knew that he hadn't been a particularly perfect gentleman himself, but he had mellowed with age and had found a wife who loved him and helped him smooth out the rough edges. Then the birth of his daughter had finished the job. Even though Pete tried to keep up the tough exterior of a policeman, he had become a softy inside. Frank, however, had had no such conversion. It seemed the older Frank got, the more like his father he became.

At first glance, the reports looked rather routine. The fire marshal's report looked clean, but Pete wasn't naive enough to assume that it was as it appeared. The Benson influence in the Panhandle of Florida was notorious. Once after a fraternity keg party, Frank had boasted about his father's "arrangement" with certain law enforcement officials. Frank had even hinted at the "financial incentives" he had given to a certain accident victim. Then with the fire, the child's disappearance, and some other related details starting to pop up, Pete was even more suspicious.

Sue Ellen was glad to host Hank Thomas. He was about the same age as her lawyer son, so she transferred her motherly attention to the young police officer.

"Let me get you some fresh-squeezed orange juice, Officer Thomas," Sue Ellen cooed.

"Hank."

Sue Ellen nodded. "So what do you two sleuths have planned for today?"

"Miz Anderson and I have a few more places to visit today. We have a new lead we want to follow," Hank said as Sue Ellen cut a huge slice of quiche and put it on Hank's plate.

"That's so exciting. Anything we can do to help?" Sue Ellen didn't want to come right out and ask about the new lead, but she planned to probe just enough to get the general picture. Then she would imagine the rest.

Ian moaned when he saw the water on the floor. Apparently he hadn't been careful after his daily spa baths. If only he'd noticed the trail he'd left behind him. Using one of the driest towels he had hung on the doorknob, he tried to soak up the water. *Dry, dry/Try not to cry.* The rhymes were coming regularly. In fact, Ian was starting to sleep less and worry more. He wrangled with his options constantly, weighing the consequences of each one. If he turned himself in to authorities, he might get sentenced to prison. But he might find mercy in the courts, in which case he could get sent to a foster home or juvenile home. These two options would depend on whether he was found guilty of burning down the house. Of course, he could find out that he hadn't started the fire at all, in which case he could be set free to go back to live with Aunt Jo. Or he could run farther away and spend the rest of his days living by his wits until he was old enough to defend himself. He went through these options over and over, rehearsing each one. Still, he didn't know which carried the greatest risk.

"Pastor, we had that roof redone right before you came," Deacon Spivey told his pastor.

"Really?"

"Yes, we took up an offering to fix the place up some so you'd come," the old deacon laughed. "It worked too, I guess. I suppose it's possible, but not too likely, we have a leak."

"So, where could the water have come from up near the baptistery?" Jim asked.

"I don't know, but I'll check it out this afternoon if you like. Have you asked George about it?"

Frank couldn't remember when he had been so tired, but he couldn't go home until he found Ian Lane.

"Here we go," Frank said, cranking the car that was parked just around the corner from Sue Ellen's house. Frank was glad that he'd rented a car instead of driving his own around town. Josephine Anderson would have recognized his big black sedan, and it could tip her off that he was doing the same thing as she. The Ford Escort was a bland gray and basically disappeared into the environment.

As he followed Jo and her new investigation partner, Frank thought again about what he would do if he came in contact with Ian. His father had given him the name of someone in the Mobile area that had done some "work" for him in the past. Frank reluctantly had checked to see if the man was still "in the business," remembering that his father had said that this person could act quickly and quietly on short notice. However, Frank hoped that he wouldn't have to go that far. He drove on, thinking of the casualties his father had already created. He hoped he could think of another way to silence the boy.

"I'm really not so good at reading maps, Hank, but I'll do my best," Jo said, trying to figure out where they were in the city.

"We'll figure it out together."

"Thank you so much for taking off time from the force to do this. If we don't find Ian soon . . . ," Jo said.

"Miz Anderson, I have a feeling we're gonna find Ian. I believe there have been enough prayers sent up for him and us that God's gonna protect that boy until we can get to him." Hank smiled, trying to put Jo's mind at ease.

Jo looked at the map and wiped away a tear. "Well, where shall we go first?"

"Maybe we ought to start from the bridge where we saw Mock yesterday," Hank suggested. "Of course, he said he didn't stay in one area. That's how these guys do, I've heard. Move around so that the authorities can't keep up with them."

"Guess our police force doesn't deal too much with homelessness, huh?" Jo asked.

"Most of the drifters we find are just passing through going to somewhere else. We encounter vagrancy around the train tracks. Most of them are waiting for a freight to come along so they can hitch a ride. Sometimes we'll hear about a guy over at the bus station trying to bum food or even a ticket to the next town, but mostly this kind of homelessness you find in the larger cities," Hank said. Jo was so proud of Hank's accomplishments. He had had a tough childhood. Orphaned, just like Ian, he'd been bounced around between foster homes before being taken in by his grandmother in Crestview. Maybe that was why Hank had such an interest in this case and why he had so much compassion for Ian.

"Yes, I've heard Brother Brewton talk about transients coming by the church all the time wanting a meal or a bus ticket," Jo remembered, "but, you know, I never remember actually talking to one of them."

There was silence in the car. Both Hank and Jo realized that they had been so focused on their task of finding Ian that they had overlooked the obvious needs of their recent acquaintance, Jeremiah Mock.

Pete's source in Tallahassee confirmed his suspicions. The accident that Charles Benson had been involved in with Ed Lane was a starting point. The rest unfolded on the same database where Hank Thomas had gotten his information. The only difference was that Pete had a little more "pull" than Hank with law enforcement even across state lines. A few favors called in and a few high school football buddies who knew people, and Pete was getting a clear picture of what the Benson family could do. Of course, Pete was careful to probe where he wouldn't leave his own trail.

"They don't tell us to think much around here,

Lieutenant. They want us to react quickly," the fireman said over the phone.

Pete's trail had led him back to the Madison Fire Department and one Walter Patton. "Tell me what happened that night, Walter. Tell me everything you know about the fire, the Lanes, and the Benson family."

Walter hesitated as if he were truly trying to think how to say what he knew. "Well, uh, is there sometime I can call you back? You know, when it's more . . . private?" he asked.

"Sure, man, anytime you like. I'm here at the station until after five. You can either call me here or after hours on my cell. Here are the numbers . . ."

Walter mumbled something and quickly hung up. It sounded to Pete like Walter knew something but was hesitant to talk about it openly. Pete hoped that the fireman would call him back and give him some perspective on the case. Just as Pete was hanging up, a secretary buzzed in. "Lieutenant, there's a Frank Benson on the line."

"No, sir, Preacher. I haven't been up there in awhile. Haven't had a need to, really. Matter of fact, I was gonna go up and check on the baptistery this afternoon to make sure it was okay for baptizing Sunday," George told Jim.

"Let's go up together. I'll show you where I saw the water," Jim said.

Ian hadn't planned on having more company. In fact, he had planned to venture out after George's afternoon cleaning. Ian was getting really hungry, and he had finished off all his stash of food, including the crackers, and most of the peanut butter and grape juice. And he still needed to drain the spa. When Ian heard the two men walking up the stairs and down the hallway toward him, his heart pounded and he rolled himself into a tight ball again. This time he prayed. Nothing elaborate, but a mere silent *Help me* was his plea.

"I don't understand it. It's dry as a bone now," Jim said, seeing no evidence of the water he'd seen before.

"And there's no stains or nothing on the ceiling, Preacher. Say you saw water on the floor here?" George asked.

"Yes. Right here." Jim pointed.

"Well, it's gone now," George said, holding a flashlight that was scanning the ceiling and the floor space.

"Maybe it was my imagination." Mercy and Hope meowed. Apparently they had followed the men.

Ian tightened every muscle, careful not to make any noise.

"While I'm up here, I'll check the baptistery. Need to start it filling."

"Good." The pastor sounded distracted, like he was still looking for the water source.

Just then Ian saw a fuzzy paw swatting at him under the door. Apparently the cats suspected Ian's presence there. How did they know? *No, no/Go, go!/No, no/Go, go.* Ian's mind raced and his heart pounded wildly.

"Oh, yeah, George—" Apparently the pastor hadn't noticed the cat's discovery. Either that or he had another thought. "We're needing some more towels in the men's robing room. And do you think we can get a small robe for Hunter?"

"Sure. I think there's some more towels in a closet in the basement. Might need to go down to the bookstore to get the robe, though," George answered.

"I've gotta go down there for something else. I'll just pick one up then."

"Haven't needed baptism supplies much in the last years. Now that you're here . . ." The men's voices faded, and the cats apparently followed them down the stairs.

Ian was relieved that George had forgotten to fill the "baptistery," as he called it. Ian knew that he wouldn't be able to hide his presence much longer. If he could survive another day, he felt he'd have to run away.

After the building was quiet, Ian ventured out at dusk to find food, but before he went, he opened the drain to his spa and rhymed his good-bye to this luxury he had discovered.

Water, water, go down the drain
When will you ever come again?

Hank and Jo had looked for a cemetery near a playground and had totally struck out. They called Sue Ellen to see if she could think of any such combination, a private burial ground near a playground. Even Sue Ellen didn't think of her own church.

The church play area had not been used very often. In fact, it could hardly be considered a playground. It had one swing set, which was in need of repair. The few children who attended the church weren't encouraged to play there. It was feared that the equipment was too old for safety, so the area was basically off-limits to the children. Overgrown shrubbery covered the area, so few ever thought about it. The cemetery wasn't used very often either. It mostly had the remains of long-forgotten church members—and now a fresh grave with the body of a child named James Copeland.

Weary and discouraged, Jo and Hank soothed their woes with Tibby's beignets and café au lait.

"You not find de boy, huh?" Tibby said, pouring coffee and hot milk into large mugs.

"No, we're looking for a cemetery near a playground, Mr. Thibodeaux," Jo said. "That's where the homeless man said he'd seen Ian."

"A boy who fits Ian's description," Hank corrected.

"Huh." Tibby thought for a second. "There's that old cemetery next to the church, you know."

"But there's not a playground, is there?" Jo asked.

"Not really," Tibby answered. "Just an old swing set, I think, back dere. Nobody use it anymore."

"It's worth checking out." Hank said.

"It would be a little too much of a coincidence, I'm thinking," Jo said with a shrug.

Pete didn't usually work late on Friday afternoons, but he lingered a little longer over paperwork, hoping that the fireman from Madison would call. When Walter called, Pete was glad he had waited.

"I really didn't know what to do, Lieutenant." The fire-fighter sounded a little frightened.

"You're doing the right thing, Mr. Patton." Pete scrambled for a pad and pencil.

Pete Lambert wasn't truly surprised to hear what Walter had to say. In fact, it put all the pieces together. It seemed that an anonymous caller had called the firemen to the burning house. By the time Walter and his buddy Andy reached the house, it was too far gone to enter. It was fully engulfed and hotter than any fire Walter could remember.

"A faulty-wiring fire would have probably started in the attic, in which case it would have smoldered and smoked for a while," Walter continued. "Even though the Lanes were notorious drunks, I think they would have heard smoke alarms. At least the boy would have."

"It had smoke detectors?" Pete asked, writing furiously.

"Oh, yeah. But . . ." Walter paused.

"But what?"

"They didn't have batteries."

Pete couldn't believe what he was hearing. "You mean they had been disarmed?"

"Yeah."

"But that's not in the fire marshal's report."

"I know. I guess it's possible that the Lanes had done it themselves, but . . ."

"Yeah. Why? What else, Walter?"

"Well, I'm not a genius, but I know a suspicious fire when I see one. The pattern of it just made me think that the source was external," Walter said carefully.

"You mean arson," Pete responded flatly.

"That's what I'm saying."

The rest of the conversation made Pete nauseous. He knew that his buddy Frank had a shady family connection, but he was shocked to hear of the suspicious deaths of the two men, Nick and Trooper.

"Have you talked to authorities about this, Walter?"

"Well, sir, the official reports of the fire, the deaths, even the car wreck involving Mr. Benson and the Lanes don't say a word about what I believe to be the truth," Walter explained.

"So you don't feel as though you have enough evidence to go to authorities. Is that right?"

"Yes, sir. I don't know who else out there thinks like me,

but so much of this don't add up."

"Or maybe it adds up to several federal crimes," Pete said.

Ian really had nothing to lose. He raided the kitchen one last time, not being so careful to leave the pantry and the refrigerator looking undisturbed. Finding a plastic grocery sack under the sink, he filled it with more crackers, his leftover peanut butter, a half of a box of Girl Scout cookies, and a clean knife. He also took a paper bag with pastries in it. He knew he could survive for a while on that. Looking around the kitchen, he felt a little sad leaving the place. It had been home to him for almost two weeks. Ian had no idea where he'd go or how he'd get there, but when he closed the basement door behind him one last time, he silently thanked God for helping him find this place.

The door locked, and Ian went out on his own into the world.

Chapter Twenty-Two

Abbie felt like it was old times, seeing Jim sitting at his desk at 3 A.M. "Something the matter, honey?" Abbie asked softly.

"No, not really. I'm just thinking."

Abbie knew better. So many times she had seen her husband wrestle with a problem or a decision. He'd think and pray until dawn, she figured.

"Anything specific I can help you with?"

Jim paused and looked at his wife. "Well, maybe. Miss Sue Ellen called and told me that her friend, Mrs. Anderson, and a policeman from Madison had some new information about that runaway boy. They told me that they had found the homeless guy who had said he'd made contact with the runaway nephew of Mrs. Anderson." Jim looked as if he were calculating in his mind as he spoke.

"To tell you the truth, I didn't believe that the guy had seen the boy. Some of the men who come by the church looking for a handout don't look like they could identify themselves, much less anybody else. A couple of weeks ago real early on a Saturday, this guy bangs on the front door wanting food. I didn't have anything, but I gave him pocket change. . . ." Jim paused as if he had discovered something.

"What is it?" Abbie asked drowsily.

"A playground . . . a cemetery . . . the water on the floor . . . my cake went missing . . . and the cats today were . . ." Jim seemed to be babbling, but Abbie was used to it.

Jim looked at his wife. "Honey, go back to bed. I won't rest until I check something out."

Abbie shrugged and shuffled back to their bedroom.

Jim entered from the basement door, remembering that at one time earlier that week, the door lock had been repaired. It was like a revelation. The refrigerator had been somewhat bare over the last few days, so there was nothing to steal, but Jim opened it just to look anyway. As he had remembered, the refrigerator was pretty empty. First, he looked around in the basement. Both the ladies' and men's rest rooms were as they should be. None of the classrooms looked out of the ordinary. Ascending the stairs, Jim had a thought, one that made him light-headed and giddy. Wouldn't it be amazing if the missing boy, identified by the homeless man, sought after by friends of his own church members, had actually hidden out in *his* church?

Jim ran the rest of the way up the stairs. But when he entered the sanctuary, he decided to approach quietly so he wouldn't scare the boy, if indeed he was there.

Pete couldn't sleep. The information that rolled over in his head pointed to Frank Benson and his family being involved in crimes so heinous that Pete, who thought he'd seen everything, was sickened. If all the evidence and witnesses could be gathered, Lieutenant Peter Lambert could send his old college buddy and his father to the penitentiary for the rest of their lives.

Ian didn't know how far he'd walked. He just knew he was tired. He also knew he'd have to find a hiding place when the sun came up. Then, perhaps during the next night he could find a way to get out of town.

The back steps creaked, even though Jim tried hard to be quiet. If the child was up in one of the abandoned rooms, Jim didn't want to frighten him. Slowly he approached the closed doors behind the pulpit. He was glad he had remembered to bring a flashlight, because he hadn't been in that part of the building enough to know where the light switches were.

Jim decided to try all the doorknobs on the hallway. The first one was locked, and Jim was pretty sure the boy wouldn't be in there anyway. Using his master key, Jim opened the door. Then he remembered. This closet was where the Lord's Supper silver and other valuables were kept.

The next doors were baptismal preparation rooms. He had just seen these that day. Both were as he had left them, except that the men's room had a few fresh towels lying in a stack on a shelf. Apparently George had found some extras. That reminded him. He'd need to bring the small robe he had bought that day for the little candidate.

The next doors were rest rooms. The ladies' room was equipped with two hair dryers, the men's with one. Nothing looked out of the ordinary.

Finally, the last door, the organ chamber, the door where he had seen Mercy and Hope playing. A broken chair, some flower arrangements, and a stack of old hymnals lined the hallway to the room. He squeezed past the forgotten items through a tiny path down the center of the hall.

Slowly, Jim approached the room. He wasn't sure what he hoped to find—an empty room or a missing child. If the child were there, Jim prayed that he'd be alive and well, and not too frightened.

He took a deep breath and turned the knob. At first, the chamber looked empty and Jim almost sighed in relief. However, when he shined his flashlight into one corner, he was shocked at what he found.

The idea of hiding out in a church appealed to Ian. He had found comfort and sustenance at the last place. He had also had a front-row seat to the lives of the people who attended there. Ian thought about Pastor Jim and Abbie. He thought about the little baby they had lost. He thought about George and Hope and Mercy and all the people who were now familiar faces to him. Suddenly he missed them. And then he had a thought: *Do those people act the same way outside the church as they do inside? Do they care for each other, console each other, smile at each other, and feed each other in the world out there?* He so hoped that they did. He knew that the world he had lived in for ten years before had had its good and bad people, and he liked to think that the good ones were those who attended churches like the one that had been his home.

Ian dashed between alleys and buildings in the dark, looking for some place that had a church symbol. His former home had had a cross on the lighted sign. He had learned that a cross was an identification that related to Jesus. The books he had read mostly had Jesus helping people and doing good things. However, one of them told a story of how the Man had been unjustly accused and had been cruelly killed by being nailed to a cross. Ian didn't like that book, but it helped him to understand a little more about the Man and His Father.

There were school buildings, government buildings, houses, and stores, but for a long way he did not see a church building.

Finally, out in a clearing, he spotted a large building that had a huge lighted cross on the top of a pointed spire. He almost ran to it, hoping to find safety. But he walked slowly in among the shadows so as not to draw attention to himself.

There were no unlocked doors in the church building. Not one. He tried them all, turning each knob and then pushing with all his strength, thinking that by a fluke the lock would have been broken as he had found before.

This church was totally different from his former church. This building was new, red brick with large white columns on the front porch. The lawn was perfectly manicured, and the parking lot looked like it had been freshly striped. There was a large, well-equipped playground inside a fence, and Ian let himself into it.

Ian figured it was an hour or so until dawn. He opened his food sack and helped himself to a modest helping of peanut butter on crackers but not before he had eyed a working water fountain near the playground.

Jo was already awake when the phone rang at Sue Ellen's. She didn't answer it but waited until Sue Ellen picked up the receiver back in her bedroom. *An early morning phone call is usually bad news or a wrong number,* she thought. Jo prayed for the wrong number option.

"Josephine. Hank. Get up!" Sue Ellen was practically floating through the house, struggling to get her bathrobe on and tied around her.

Hank stuck his head out of a bedroom. Jo grabbed her robe and ran into the hall. Jean, who was not quite awake yet, raised up out of the sofa bed she and Jo had shared since Hank arrived.

"What? What is it?" Jo asked.

"Everybody get dressed, right now. That was my pastor. He said he found something at the church he thinks relates to Ian."

Sue Ellen wanted Hank to drive her Cadillac. She was just too nervous, so nervous that she realized ten miles into the trip that she still had her hair net on. Taking the net off, she freed the pin curls from their bobby pins and tried to fluff her coiffure.

"Tell me exactly what the pastor told you, Sue Ellen," Jo said from the backseat. She leaned forward and lightly punched at Sue Ellen's hair.

"He said that he had found a small room, a closet really, that looked like somebody had been living there, a small somebody, a child probably. Judging from the bedding, the food wrappings, and the books he found in a stack, it had been a rather tidy child."

"That's Ian!" Jo gasped.

"And you said it was too much of a coincidence," Jean yawned from the opposite corner of the backseat.

"Did he call the police?" Jo asked.

"I am the police," Hank said playfully.

"I know, Hank, but did he call local police?"

"I hope not," Hank added.

"I don't think so, Jo. I think he called us first."

Pete didn't usually work on Saturdays, but he was so troubled by the case, he told his wife he had to put in at least a few hours going over his notes.

When his cell phone rang around eight o'clock, Pete thought it was Sandra wanting him to pick up something at the store on his way home. But it was Frank Benson.

"Sandy said you'd gone into the office early this morning," Frank said.

"Uh, yeah. I remembered I'd left some things here undone, so I thought I'd come in for a little while to tie up some loose ends," Pete answered.

"Anything I'd be interested in?"

"Oh, no, it's some break-ins we're investigating on the east side," Pete lied.

"Well, I've got some news, bro."

"What?" Pete was hoping it wasn't anything that would lead Frank to the child. A shiver went down Pete's spine as he circled the words *arson* and *murder* on the legal pad he had written on the day before.

"Saw that bum again last night."

"Really?"

"Yeah, I'd stopped into a club for a beer, and lo and

behold, if he wasn't hanging around lurking in the shadows as I left," Frank explained.

"Boy, you must have picked one of Mobile's finer clubs if that guy was a fellow patron," Pete said as he tried to lighten the mood.

"No, I said he was hanging around outside asking for a handout," Frank explained. "Anyway, I played a little 'come-and-get-it' with a ten-dollar bill, and the guy told me he remembered something else about that night he saw the kid."

"Really?" Pete was truly interested in the new information.

"He said that the playground was near a cemetery where his mother was buried."

"Yeah?"

"So all we have to do is find that info in some records somewhere, and, boom, we've found our boy."

Pete rubbed his temples and tried to think what to do. He knew he had to beat his friend to the punch and find that boy. "Uh, yeah, I'll look into it while I'm here. I'll call you when I find out something."

"I can't believe it," Jo said as they crossed into the Mobile city limits. "We were at that little graveyard yesterday, saw the Mock woman's grave, even saw the swing set behind that overgrowth, and I still didn't think that that was where the old man had seen Ian."

"Me either," Hank said. "Apparently we've been within a few feet of Ian and didn't even know it."

"Wonder if he knew we were looking for him," Jo mused out loud.

"Who knows?"

Pastor Jim Copeland was waiting on the front steps of the church when the yellow Cadillac drove up.

"Pastor, did you call anybody but us about this?" Hank asked.

"Well . . ."

"Don't! Please!" Jo pleaded.

"Why not?" the pastor asked.

Jean and Sue Ellen looked puzzled too. Apparently, there was something about this case that their friends had not told them.

"There was an officer handing out flyers here last week. I tried to call him at the police station, but he wasn't there. I left a message, though."

While Jim unlocked the front door of the church, Jo and Hank gave the others a quick rundown of the situation with Frank Benson and the danger he possibly posed to Ian. Jean shook her head, and Sue Ellen started to cry. The pastor looked concerned as he led the group up the stairs behind the pulpit and to the closet where he had not disturbed anything he had found earlier.

"It's hard to tell. There aren't any clothes or anything that Ian was wearing when he disappeared," Jo said, looking at all the contents of the small room. She stooped down and smelled the mattress; she looked inside a plastic grocery sack and found wads of saltine wrappers and two empty grape juice jars.

Hank warned, "Don't touch anything, Miz Anderson, more than you have to, I mean."

Jim began to talk about all the other clues that had led him to this discovery, the broken lock, the stolen cake, the mysterious appearance and disappearance of standing water, the cats' behavior.

"Pastor, Ian could have very easily been here for a while. He had learned to take care of himself, you know. There is probably more food missing than you've realized. The water could mean that he bathed up here," Jo said.

"The baptistery," Jim said. "It's right through that door there. And yeah, for much of the last couple of weeks there has been lots of food in the fridge downstairs. We never would have missed anything, I'm sure."

Sue Ellen cried louder, "Oh, my. I cleaned out that refrigerator myself and threw away a lot of old food. If I'd known that child was surviving by eating—" Her voice trailed off. Jean tried to console her.

Jo laughed and shook her head. It was really funny to think about little Ian hiding in an organ chamber, eating scavenged food, and bathing in a baptistery.

"What's so funny?" Hank asked.

"This could only have been Ian," Jo answered, but then fear struck. "But where is he now?"

The station usually ran on a skeleton crew over the weekend. Except for an enlarged group of dispatchers, who were put on for the increased crime that was sure to happen on the weekend, there were no secretaries or other officers on Pete's hall. His intercom line rang.

"Lieutenant Lambert," Pete answered.

A weekend dispatcher was on the line.

"Lieutenant, I took a message early this morning for Officer Mixon. It was a Reverend Jim Copeland saying that he maybe had some information about a missing child. I was going to just put this on the front desk board, but since I saw you go up to your office, I thought I'd just call you about this. Don't know if it's anything . . ."

"Yes! Thank you so much. I'm glad you called. Hey, also don't relay the message to anyone else, will you?"

"Not even to Officer Mixon?" the dispatcher asked.

"Not even to Officer Mixon. This is a delicate matter, and anything like this needs to come directly to me." Before he hung up the phone, Pete added, "There's a guy named Frank Benson who might call here for me. Tell him you don't know where I am, OK?"

Remembering it was Saturday, Ian figured that no one would be coming to the church all day. Of course, he couldn't be sure of that, but he found a really good temporary hideout at the corner of the building where thick shrubs created a kind of fort. Ian piled up some pine straw that lay at the base of the shrubs and made himself a pallet of sorts. Ian was sure that it would get hot when the sun came out more. Then he realized that he hadn't been outside during the day in more than two weeks. He lay there and thought about Aunt Jo. He wondered if she had given up looking for him by now. Didn't police call off searches after a while? Maybe they thought he was dead. That thought made Ian sad, not so much for himself, but for Aunt Jo. He guessed she would be sad if he died. Then that thought made Ian think about heaven. He had heard of it and had guessed that good people would go there, but one of the books he had read during his stay at the church had said that heaven was for those who believed in Jesus. He hadn't really thought about it, but he guessed he believed in Jesus. Jesus was a good Man, God's Son, died on a cross . . . for sinners, the book had said. Sinners. Ian watched white clouds pass overhead, and lying there on his pine straw bed he realized he was a sinner. He had done wrong things. He had run away and stolen food. He had maybe even started a fire that had killed his parents. There was probably more, but wasn't that enough?

He started to cry. For the first time in a while, he cried, not because he was scared or even because he was sad. He cried because he was sorry. The tears came while he prayed. He wasn't sure God could hear him through the sobs, but he listed all the things he could remember that he had done wrong.

"I'm sorry for everything," Ian wept, feeling the sorrow down deep in the pit of his stomach.

"Reverend Copeland?" Pete said as Jim answered the cell phone.

"Yes?"

"I'm Lieutenant Peter Lambert, Mobile Police Force. A dispatcher relayed a message to me that you had left for Officer Mixon," Pete said.

Jim tried to think fast. "Oh, well, that . . ."

"I understand you may have some new information on Ian Lane's disappearance."

"I'm sorry, Lieutenant, I'm getting another call. Can you hang on?" Jim chided himself silently for not thinking of a better response. He punched the "mute" button on his phone. "This is a Lieutenant Lambert from Mobile Police Force. Apparently he's following up on the message I left Officer Mixon. What do I tell him?" Jim asked Hank.

"Tell him it was a mistake and that you will call him if you find something."

Jim nodded and repeated what Hank had told him word for word.

Pete thanked the pastor, but he didn't believe Jim's response. *It wouldn't take much of a detective to find a Reverend Jim Copeland in the city,* Pete thought.

A phone call or two and Pete knew exactly where Broad Street Church was located.

Lying behind the shrubbery in the straw, Ian thought about baby Jesus lying in straw. The thought made him feel a little better, and the tears stopped. He was thankful that the corner he had chosen was shaded and cool, and for several hours, he slept more peacefully than ever.

Jo stayed up in the organ chamber, sitting on the pallet Ian had left. Hank took a seat on the front pew. Jean and Sue Ellen sat together holding hands on a back pew. Jim paced back and forth on the platform. They all prayed, sometimes aloud, sometimes silently, sometimes crying; but all were asking God for wisdom, for guidance, and for safety to find the lost boy soon. Jim had called Abbie and asked her to pray also.

"Perfect love casteth out fear," Jim murmured, when the passage in 1 John came to his mind. "Greater is he that is in you than he that is in the world." It was another promise that Jim was claiming from the same Book.

"Give Your angels charge over him, God," Jo said.

"The Lord is my strength," Sue Ellen repeated over and over through the tears.

Jean remembered Isaiah, "When thou passest through the waters, I will be with thee: and through the rivers, they shall not overflow thee: when thou walkest through the fire, thou shalt not be burned; neither shall the flame kindle thee."

Abbie read aloud from Psalm 91: "He that dwelleth in the secret place of the most High shall abide under the shadow of the Almighty. . . . He shall cover thee with his feathers, and under his wings shalt thou trust: his truth shall be thy shield and buckler. Thou shalt not be afraid for the terror by night; nor for the arrow that flieth by day.'"

Hank added a petition to God for a spirit of peace for Josephine Anderson. It was the least he could do for the saint who had led him to Christ.

It was a prayer vigil as none of them had experienced before. It was a time, rare they all knew, when they felt totally helpless, and when their only recourse was to surrender the situation totally to the only One who could help, the only One who could be trusted. It could have been hours that they were there. No one knew or cared about the time.

Suddenly Jim's countenance changed. His petition ceased and he began to listen. Just listen.

"There are many who are lost. Do not forget them. I have not." Jim heard the voice as clear as day. He opened his eyes to see who had spoken. He saw the others in the room still engaged in prayer. Jim realized that he had heard God speak in a voice that only he had heard.

He loved the sound of His voice. He asked God to speak again. But there was silence.

Jim asked what it meant. *"There are many who are lost.*

Do not forget them. I have not." The statements were indelibly etched on his heart, but he asked for their meaning and application. Still there was silence.

The serenity of the vigil was interrupted by the sound of a cellular phone ringing in the foyer.

Frank was getting really annoyed. He must have called the police station, Pete's home, and Pete's cell phone ten times in three hours. Sandra said that she hadn't heard from her husband since early that morning. The dispatcher had no idea where the lieutenant had gone but offered repeatedly to put Frank through to Pete's voice mail. Frank left one message and then refused the other times. Pete didn't seem to be answering his cell phone either.

Frank decided to strike out on his own, to go to every cemetery/playground combination in Mobile—in the state if he had to. But he was determined to silence Ian Lane before he told anybody what he knew.

Ian's nap was interrupted by the sound of someone yelling. Peeking through the thick shrubbery, Ian watched as several teenagers got off a bus that had just pulled up. It looked as if the teenagers had been on an overnight trip, because they were unloading backpacks and sleeping bags. They also looked as though they hadn't slept much. A few of the girls got off the bus with pillows and tousled hairdos that made it look like they had made a futile attempt at sleeping on the return trip. All of the teenagers looked like they were tired, except for a few of the younger teenage boys. They were the ones who were yelling and chasing each other in the parking lot.

A young man called for all the teenagers to form a circle. Dropping pillows and backpacks, the teenagers complied. They all joined hands while the young man prayed out loud.

Ian was glad to see people praying outside the church. And the teenagers looked as though they cared about each other and about the young man who led them. It was this kind of love he had seen at Broad Street, and he suddenly wanted to go back there.

After the teenagers left and the bus pulled away, Ian wondered if he could retrace his steps from the night before. He had dashed in and out of alleys and down dark streets so many times that he wasn't so sure how to get back to his former home. All he knew to do then was to say, "God, help me."

Pete apologized for the intrusion.

"Can I help you?" Jim Copeland asked. Jo walked down the steps and into the sanctuary.

"I'm Lieutenant Pete Lambert, Mobile Police Department," Pete said.

Hank looked at Jim. Jim continued the lead. "Yes, I talked to you on the phone today."

"You did."

Hank stepped forward. "I'm Hank Thomas, police officer from Crestview." Hank wanted to make sure that Pete knew that they weren't defenseless, that there was another official authority present.

Pete shook Hank's hand. "Have you found evidence of

the boy?" Pete asked.

Jim looked at Hank, who looked at Jo.

Pete figured that they would be a little skeptical of his presence. "I have to tell you that I know more about this case than you might think. In fact, I know about the danger that Ian may be in. I know Frank Benson personally." Jim and Hank exchanged glances of alarm. "I assure you I am not working with him. In fact, I'm onto him. Please, can you tell me where the boy is?"

Jim answered, "No, we can't."

Pete protested, "Reverend, I'm not here to harm the child."

"I understand. But we don't know where Ian is." Jim paused and looked at the others. "However, we believe that he was here in this building for some time. We don't think he's been gone very long, but we don't know where he is. We were just praying about it, asking God's guidance and protection."

Pete blushed and said an uncomfortable "I see."

"What do you know about Frank Benson, Lieutenant?" Hank asked. And they all sat on the front pew and exchanged information about the fire, the deaths of Nick and Trooper, and the history of the Benson influence.

Ian wondered if it would be better to find his way back in the dark. That was how he had come, so maybe the path would look more familiar at night. At dusk, he began to walk away from the big church and down the sidewalk he had traveled the night before.

Ian was surprised that he remembered so many landmarks. Fast-food restaurants dotted his course. He had been hungry before, and he salivated at what he smelled.

The place that sold boats looked right too. He had remembered his favorite poem "Where Go the Boats?" when he had passed it. He was confident he was going the right way. An overpass looked familiar too. The graffiti on the bridge had been memorable, but he was ashamed to admit he recognized the dirty words written there.

A long row of houses came into view. Each house had a fence around it, and they were very close together. He remembered the street vividly. The night before, he had heard yelling coming from inside one of the houses. Then he had heard yelling from some of the surrounding houses for the people in that house to stop yelling. He had remembered too that the language was mostly angry vulgarity. This had taken him back to memories of his parents. The sight of the house on his return trip made him sad again.

The street ended, and he had to make a decision about which way he should turn. Neither looked familiar. To the right were more houses. To the left looked like a main thoroughfare with businesses and moderately heavy traffic. He stopped to think. Finally he remembered seeing a tattoo parlor somewhere along the way. He figured he would have better luck finding such an establishment if he went toward the business section. Of course, if the tattoo parlor didn't appear pretty soon, he would turn back the other way. Fortunately, the tattoo parlor and a pawnshop were just as he had remembered, and he thought that next would be open field. He was right. The sun was setting just on the other side of a grassy meadow he recognized.

As he walked, Ian's footsteps fell into a rhythm. Ordinarily he would have made up a rhyme to the beat, but this time he felt as though he didn't really need a rhyme. He did, however, repeat silently a prayer he remembered. *Where can I go?*

Frank was glad that he had decided not to turn in his rental car. He was glad because of who he saw walking down a dark street.

"I can dispatch several units to cruise the city," Pete offered. "They can be instructed to not approach the boy, if you think it'd spook him."

Hank thought that it was a good idea, but Jo had some reservations. "Didn't you say that Frank had a police scanner?"

"That's right." Pete remembered that he was the one who had shared that information. "I really think that Frank would do harm to the boy if he found him."

Jo moved to a back pew and began to pray again. Sue Ellen and Jean joined her.

Pete leaned in and said to Hank, "I'm not sure what good they think that'll do. You don't just sit here and pray and—poof!—the boy returns."

Hank tried not to be harsh. It was apparent that Pete didn't feel comfortable even standing inside a church building, much less talking about a believer's prayer. "That's all they can do for a lost boy right now," Hank explained.

The words echoed inside Jim's head. *There are many who are lost. Do not forget them. I have not.* This is what God's voice had said, and now the meaning was starting to come clear.

"Lieutenant, I know where they serve the best beignets this side of New Orleans. Care to join me?" Jim asked. Almost as if it had been choreographed, Hank joined the ladies in prayer. Pete shrugged and realized it had been several hours since he had eaten.

Ian was proud of his memory. He seemed to be following his former trail perfectly. The schoolhouse was coming up on the right. Across the street was a house with a white fence around it. Next to that house would be another made of brick with a stone statue on the lawn. The landmarks were lining up. But suddenly there was something not so perfect. It was just a feeling that Ian had. Looking behind him, he saw nothing but abandoned sidewalks. He continued walking but couldn't shake the feeling that he was not safe.

At the next cross street, Ian felt as though he should turn right. However, the dark emptiness of that street made him make another decision. He thought he should stay straight and walk toward the lights.

Frank passed the boy from behind, but he did not drive slowly. Staying with the speed limit, Frank only gave a quick glance Ian's way. It was the boy, all right, walking contentedly down a city street. At the next corner, Frank turned left and then doubled back.

"Where have you been, boy?" Frank whispered out loud as he passed Ian going the other way. Frank remembered how he detested his father calling him "boy." It was not an evil term, but it was a reference to the authority that a man can have over a boy. In a second, Frank was able to transfer the power his father had had over him to the power he would soon have over Ian.

After one more pass, Frank pulled his car into the parking lot of a convenience store and fumbled around in the backseat for his scanner. *Maybe this thing wasn't such a bad idea after all,* he thought.

Frank tuned the channel to a local frequency, one that Pete had given him, and listened for anything about a runaway boy. There was a shooting, a drug deal, a home invasion, but nothing about a boy.

Ian glanced over at Frank's car as he passed in front of the convenience store. Frank slumped down in the seat. He was certain that Ian would not recognize him in the rental car. It seemed as though Ian indeed had not recognized Frank, because the boy kept walking at his usual pace.

"These are good, Reverend," Pete said as he bit into a hot French pastry.

"Jim. You can call me Jim."

Tibby's usually closed at 6:00 on Saturdays, but he was willing to stay open longer for Brother Jim and the policeman.

"Are you from Mobile, Lieutenant?" Jim asked.

"Pete."

Jim had been invited to return a friendlier greeting.

"Sure. Pete," Jim said.

Jim didn't know where the conversation would lead, but he prayed that he could have the opportunity and the courage to share Christ with Pete.

The boy was not too hard to follow. He seemed to be

staying in lighted, busy areas. He also looked as though he knew where he was going.

I don't know where I'm going, God, but I guess You do, Ian said silently as he looked down briefly at his own feet and wondered where they were leading him.

There was nothing familiar about the stores, the houses, the streets that he passed; however, it did seem for some reason as if he were on the right track. And so he kept moving forward.

Ordinarily, Sue Ellen would have been fretting over something to do with food. Usually her goal was to make sure that the whole world was fed and happy. Jo had the same reputation and inner drive. But there was a greater task at hand. Remembering the New Testament story of Mary and Martha, the two sisters who argued about what was more important, cooking for the Master or worshiping Him, Jo dismissed the thoughts of food preparation and was content to sit at the feet of Jesus along with her three friends. No one seemed to miss the meals they had skipped that day. And so they kept praying.

Pete's cell phone did not ring, and no other patrons came into Tibby's, so Jim began to talk about his relationship with God. The police lieutenant did not look into Jim's eyes, but he seemed to be listening.

"I grew up in a rough neighborhood. I developed this

tough shell around me, you know, kind of macho, but inside I was a little scared boy. Didn't have time for church or God or anything. I was too busy having a good time. Got mixed up in a gang . . ." As the pastor continued, Pete could hardly believe his ears. The mild-mannered clergyman sitting in front of him didn't look at all like the gang members he had seen. Pete couldn't even imagine Jim Copeland as anything but a preacher.

Pete began to identify with Jim. He had not had much time for God either, especially in his college days. Pete Lambert had been known as quite the party animal. In fact, the only frat brother he had had that could drink him under the table had been Frank Benson, he remembered. That was really the only thing that Pete had admired about Frank— his ability to hold his liquor. He had always thought of Frank Benson, as everyone else had, as an arrogant rich kid who had no moral convictions at all.

When Pete had graduated from college, he decided to live a better life, get a respectable job, marry a nice girl, and settle down. So far, life had been pretty good to him. He had just made lieutenant and had a beautiful daughter. Still, however, there was something inside him that was thirsty.

The grocery store was pretty full of people. Each checkout line was at least two or three carts deep. Ian tried not to look anyone in the eye. He was still not sure if he should turn himself in or let himself be caught. A large sign said "Rest rooms," and Ian washed his face and hands in the men's room. He was glad there was no one in the stalls next to him, or they might have been suspicious about the noises he was making as he spread peanut butter on some crackers.

The taste was good, but he was more interested in the strength they would provide. For dessert, he crammed two Girl Scout cookies in his mouth almost at once and chewed them as he walked out of the stall.

The water from the fountain outside the rest room was cold and refreshing. It had been a long time since Ian had had his thirst quenched so thoroughly.

A pay phone hung on the wall. For a moment, Ian thought about calling Aunt Jo. Two things stood in his way, however: He didn't know her number, and he did not have any money. Suddenly a smell got his attention. Looking down an aisle, he could see a lady serving small slices of pizza. He remembered that the grocery store in Madison used to give away samples of new products, and he had learned to do his shopping on certain days.

Frank knew he had seen the boy go into the store, but he had lost sight of him in the crowd. Thinking that maybe the boy had been onto him, Frank drove around the parking lot a few times and looked closely at the back door and the loading dock. He waited for a while to see if Ian had tried to give him the slip.

The pizza was delicious, and the kind lady giving out samples gave him three slices. Going back to the water fountain for one last drink, Ian walked out the front door of the store and continued down the street in the same direction he had been following.

Finally, Frank gave up his idea of Ian slipping out the back door, and he drove back around to the front parking lot and waited. Ten minutes passed, and Frank was starting to get impatient. Grabbing a baseball cap he had put in the car in case he needed a disguise, Frank decided he'd go in and look around for the boy.

Walking every aisle, he saw no sign of Ian. The child was

not in the rest rooms either.

He swore under his breath and ran back to his rental car. Peeling out of the parking lot, Frank was glad that he was angry. That would make what he had to do easier.

The lights had run out, but Ian kept walking along the dark street. There was nothing else he could do. A car approached from behind, and for some reason Ian felt compelled to duck behind a car parked on the street. The car slowed down, and Ian remained still, resisting the urge to take a peek at the driver. The car drove on.

Jim knew that Tibby needed to close the bakery, so he paid for their pastries and coffee and escorted Pete to the door.

"Thank you, uh, Jim. I'll remember this place," Pete said, shaking Jim's hand.

"You're welcome to come back to the church and join us," Jim said.

"Well, I need to get home. I told my wife I'd be home for lunch." Pete looked at his watch. "Guess I missed that by about seven hours."

"Sure. I understand. You're welcome anytime at our church. We meet Sundays at 11:00 A.M. and 6:00 P.M. We have a midweek prayer service on Wednesdays too. Bring your wife and daughter. We'd love to have you," Jim said smiling.

"Thank you, Jim. We might just do that," Pete smiled back. "I promise I'll let you know if I hear anything."

Jim waggled his cell phone. "Me too. I'm always here."

Jim felt a little guilty that he hadn't fasted as the others had. They were still praying when he entered the building.

239

The more Frank drove, the angrier he got. He intermingled, "Where are you, boy?" with every expletive he could think of. Still, there was no sign of the boy. He couldn't believe that a scrawny ten-year-old had somehow defied his grasp.

Pete knew that he couldn't avoid Frank Benson anymore, so when the phone rang, Pete answered it.

"Where have you been? I've been calling you all day," Frank ranted.

"Well, I've been out. Didn't have my phone and . . ." Pete fished for the right explanation.

"Sandy didn't even know where you were."

"I was called out on a case, Frank. I can't be everywhere. Hey, Repeat, what if we meet for a drink somewhere, huh? I'm buying." Pete tried to lighten the mood and perhaps keep Frank from knowing where he'd been.

"I don't have time for a drink. I've seen the boy, Pete," Frank said.

Pete almost overreacted. "Seen the boy? Where?"

"I'm not sure where I am now . . . and I've lost him temporarily."

"I can get a unit around there in minutes . . ."

"No! Don't want to spook the kid. I think he'd be more likely to come to me than to a perfect stranger, especially a cop."

Pete wasn't sure what to do. "Tell me where you are, man, and I'll come help you."

Frank gave him street signs and landmarks, and Pete knew exactly where he was. He knew that he had promised to call Jim and the others the minute he heard about something, but if he told them that Frank Benson was on his trail, they would really worry, maybe even panic. He figured they were better off keeping their prayer vigil while he became the boy's protector.

Two men got out of their cars, talked for a few seconds, and then both got into one car. Ian couldn't see their faces at all, but he instinctively hid behind a bush when they drove by. Thankfully, the car was traveling in the opposite direction from the way he was going. Nothing was looking familiar. And he was not able to even gauge how far he had walked. He had traveled through some commercial and some residential areas without recognizing a single thing. Ian stopped walking for a minute and sat down on a brick wall next to the sidewalk. "Oh, God, I hope I'm going the right way."

"Are you sure it was him, Frank?" Pete asked.

"Positive. The kid even had on the same clothes he wore two weeks ago," Frank answered.

"Wonder where he's been all this time."

"No telling. Just want to get that boy back to his dear old aunt."

Pete looked away and rolled his eyes. Suddenly he was as afraid for the boy's safety as the others had been.

"Here. Here's the grocery store I saw him in." Frank instructed Pete to drive into the parking lot. "He had been heading that way when he went in. He never came out. At least I didn't see him."

"Let's see what we can find out," Pete said, walking through the front door of the grocery store.

Pete flashed his badge at the night manager. "Did you see a little boy about ten years old, blond hair, jeans, light blue T-shirt?"

The manager shook his head and then asked an assistant manager if he'd seen the boy. The assistant manager wasn't sure that he'd seen any child of that description.

"Ask the lady in the back giving out pizza samples. She attracts kids like flies back there," the manager said. Pete didn't think that the fly analogy in a grocery store was appropriate, but he walked back to the meat department and found the sample lady. Pete showed his badge again and asked about Ian.

"Yes, a boy fitting that description was here, oh, maybe fifteen minutes ago. He looked pretty hungry, so I gave him extra. You guys wanna try some? It's a meat lover's made fresh here in our kitchen every day." She held up a small slice for the two men. They both refused.

"See, I told you he was here," Frank insisted. "Ma'am, do you know where he went?"

The lady shook her head and shrugged. "Sorry."

Pete was running over in his mind what course of action he should take. Should he arrest his friend on the spot? Knowing what he knew about Frank Benson, Pete sure had good reason. However, the evidence was circumstantial at that point. Should he try to stall and give Ian time to get away? But Pete didn't know where Ian was going. Maybe he was going back to the safety of Broad Street. Maybe he was trying to get away from the church. Should he call in other policemen to join the search? He certainly didn't want to tip off Frank about what he knew. One thing Pete did know, however; he could not let Frank Benson get his hands on Ian Lane.

"Where are we, man?" Frank asked. Pete had been driving around in circles for half an hour at least, hoping that wherever Ian was, he'd get to safety soon.

"Just cruisin' the area. Tell me if you spot anything."

Melanie drove Abbie to the church to join the vigil. Even though Abbie had not gotten out since the baby was born, she felt it would be all right, especially if Melanie helped her up the steps. She and Jim joined hands and kneeled in the center aisle.

Melanie's husband, Dan, had called Deacon Spivey and a few other men and women in the church. By nine o'clock, the church building was filled with people praying for Ian, just as they had prayed for little James.

"Looks like we've lost him, partner," Pete said, driving Frank back to his rental car.

"No, he's out there somewhere."

"Why don't you come back to the house with me? You haven't seen Sandra or Katie since you got here," Pete pleaded.

"No. I have to find that boy."

"The boy has probably bedded down in a Dumpster somewhere. You're not gonna find him tonight."

"Yeah. I guess."

"Let me call home and tell Sandra you'll come over for a beer. Katie'll probably be asleep by now, but you can look in on her. She looks like an angel when she's asleep."

Pete's wife was not particularly excited about her husband bringing an old college buddy over at that time of night. She protested, but for some reason Pete absolutely insisted. It wasn't like Pete to inconsiderately bring people home at odd hours, nor was it like him to be so insistent. She gave in, not knowing fully Pete's agenda.

All of a sudden, things started looking vaguely familiar to Ian. He remembered an appliance store that he had passed the night before. This one looked a lot like that one. Passing in front of the store, he saw himself on a TV. He was shocked. As he turned his head, he noticed that the image turned its head too. Then he waved and the image waved. Ian giggled. There was a video camera set up somewhere to delight passersby with a vision of themselves. It would have been fun to have stayed there and played the mirror game, but he knew he had to keep moving.

Parking lots, houses, stores. They were all starting to look familiar! How had he gotten back on his path? He had not made a turn of any kind, and yet he was apparently heading back where he wanted to go. He made sure he thanked God for answering his prayer.

In the distance, he could see the big highway that ran near the church. He remembered the night he had been touched on the shoulder by some unknown person and how he had spent the night out in a concrete tube in a field. He remembered the late-night raids on the refrigerator. He remembered Hope and Mercy and Pastor Jim.

His legs started to run! He dropped the plastic sack with leftover food and sprinted as fast as he could. He was going home! No matter the consequences, no matter what happened, he knew it was the right thing to do. He was not afraid. Not even a little bit.

He could see the lighted sign out in front of the church. There was the cross! He would never forget it.

Tears began to fall, and he could hardly catch his breath. He was so tired, so relieved, so sad and glad, and his heart pounded with every emotion he had ever felt.

He knew that it was Saturday night and that no one would be at the church until morning, but at least he could be waiting for them when they arrived. Maybe he could even fix up the place, pick up trash around the building, or . . .

There were cars in the parking lot, lots of cars. Had he been wrong? Was this Wednesday night? Or Sunday night? Maybe this was a funeral or a wedding. He would be very quiet, he thought. He wouldn't spoil the solemn moment. Climbing the steps, he listened for the music. There was none. He listened for the pastor's voice. He heard nothing.

He pulled on the handle of the large wooden front door and walked into the crimson-carpeted foyer. There were people inside, he could tell, but no one seemed to be saying a word. Ian stood for a moment and waited. He would go in and just sit quietly in the back until he could get the attention of the pastor or someone he recognized.

The door to the auditorium opened silently, and Ian looked at the people there. They were all praying. Some were whispering, and some were lying facedown on the floor. What were they doing? He remembered the night the people came and prayed for the baby. He wondered, had something happened to Abbie?

Ahead of him, he saw Pastor Jim kneeling on the floor. A woman sat next to him. Both of them looked intense and troubled. The pastor rocked back and forth whispering. Ian couldn't understand what he was saying, but Pastor Jim was obviously talking to God. Without thinking, Ian reached out and put his hand on the pastor's shoulder. The pastor did not open his eyes. Ian was glad that he had not disturbed the prayer.

Then Ian decided to join the prayer.

"Thank You, God, for bringing me home," Ian spoke quietly.

Jim Copeland opened his eyes. He thought it had to be a vision! He was astonished. He had heard God's voice and seen a vision all in one day. But the vision had dirty blond hair, a ragged blue T-shirt, and faded jeans.

"Pastor Jim?" Ian looked into the man's eyes and then fell into his arms.

It took a couple of seconds before the others realized what had happened. One man started to laugh out loud. A woman started to shout, "Praise God!" Somebody broke into a hymn, and Josephine Anderson began to sob as she clung with all her strength to the little boy.

"Aunt Jo?" Ian looked surprised. "What's going on?"

It took two hours for Ian to tell his story and for Aunt Jo to fill him in on their saga. Ian told them about the things he had learned about Jonah, about prayer, about Jesus, about sin. He told them all how he had cried because he was sorry. The others told him about how they had prayed for his safety and for his salvation. And finally, Jo was able to tell Ian that he was not responsible for the fire that had killed his parents. The relief brought tears to everyone's eyes again.

Finally, Hank remembered that he had told the lieutenant he would call if they heard any word about Ian. They had not only heard a word, but he was standing in their very presence!

When Pete's phone rang, he was sure that Frank was passed out on the couch. He had decided that it would be better for Frank to stay at his house for the night anyway, but Pete didn't tell Frank why.

"What? You found him where?" Pete was as astonished and elated as the church members he could hear celebrating in the background were. "That's great. Is he all right?"

Pete vowed to Hank that he would not tell Frank about Ian's reappearance. And he wouldn't. Pete knew that the boy was still not out of danger, not while Frank Benson had the boy in his sights.

"We're going to get a doctor to look him over first thing in the morning. Right now we're taking him back to Sue Ellen's to get him cleaned up and fed. I'll take them all home to Crestview tomorrow," Hank said. "We'll have to decide then what to do about the Benson case."

"Right. Thanks for calling me. Tell everyone congratulations."

The intoxicating fog was not as thick over Frank's brain as Pete had thought. In fact, Frank had heard every word.

Chapter Twenty-three

It sounded as if it were

the queen's coronation. Edwina Beck, the church organist for the past forty years, literally pulled out all the stops. The carillon bells rang out loud and clear for the first time in anyone's memory. But it was a day of celebration! A child had come home.

The news had spread by eleven o'clock, and the sanctuary was packed. All three local TV stations had camera crews and reporters, whom the ushers were trying to keep at bay until after the worship service.

The first candidate entered the water with a new robe.

"This is Hunter Gregory, who gave his life to the Lord." The pastor raised his hand. "In obedience to our Lord and Savior Jesus Christ, I baptize you, my little brother, in the name of the Father, the Son, and the Holy Ghost." Jim tipped the boy's head back and placed him under the warm water. "Buried with Him in baptism, raised to walk in a newness of life."

The next candidate entered the water with an old but freshly washed and pressed robe.

"This is Ian Lane. You all know by now this boy's journey to faith. After talking to him last night and this morning, he told me that he had repented of his sins and given his life to the Lord. Ian will not be joining our church but will be returning to Crestview with his great-aunt. But Ian said he wanted to be baptized here." Jim chuckled and spoke softly to Ian. "I know this isn't your first time in this baptistery, but this time you'll really be clean." Ian looked at the pastor and smiled.

There was not a dry eye in the room, including Ian's. His face was wet with tears, and when he was immersed, it felt as though the dirtyness of his life *was* washed away.

Jim stood Ian and Hunter side by side.

"People, here are two boys sharing the waters of baptism today. One has been in the constant care of his parents since he was born. The other has been on the run for quite some time, and many people all over the area have been searching for him. However, understand that both of them were lost. Both of them realized, perhaps by different means, that they were sinners and needed Christ. Two boys lost. Now two ambassadors for Christ going out into the world."

In the history of the little church, there had never been applause given in a worship service. However, at that moment, not only did applause erupt, but a standing ovation went on for five minutes. The two boys beamed, the pastor cried, and sobs of joy were heard all over the room.

Pete woke up and saw that Frank was not on the couch. He didn't know how long Frank had been gone, but Pete immediately threw on a T-shirt and jeans and headed to the Broad Street area.

A large crowd had gathered. The TV vans and passersby clogged the street in front of the church. Pete stopped his car on the perimeter and stood up on the running board to see over the crowd. He couldn't spot Frank anywhere. Getting back in his car, Pete called the dispatcher at the station and asked what was going on at the church. Pete was a little relieved to hear that the hubbub was about the boy's discovery and not about harm that had come to him. But Pete was still afraid of what Frank Benson might do.

"I'm sorry, sir. Mr. Benson checked out earlier this morning," the clerk at the Marriott registration desk told Pete.

"What time?" Pete asked.

"Uh . . ."

Pete flashed his badge, and the clerk felt a little more at ease and tried to remember the details of Frank's departure.

"Our checkout time is at eleven, but he called the desk around ten this morning and asked if I'd prepare his bill. I did, and within five minutes he was standing here with his luggage."

"Did he call for his car?"

"I don't know, but you can ask at the valet stand."

Frank had called for his car, and according to the valet, he had headed east out of the parking lot. "Without leaving a tip," the valet said under his breath.

"Did he say where he was going?" Pete showed his badge.

"No, sir, he didn't. Just drove off without saying a word." Pete handed the young man a five-dollar bill.

✦ ✦ ✦

Ian didn't know what to say when the news reporters rushed to him when he stepped out of the sanctuary and into the foyer.

"Where have you been, son?" "Where have your travels taken you?" "Where will you go now?"

Ian clung to Aunt Jo's hand, and she politely declined the reporters' questions. Hank walked in front of her and Ian and adapted some blocking techniques he had learned in high school football. Using his forearms and elbows, Hank was able to create a wide enough chute for Ian and his guardian to exit the foyer and descend the stairs to the dining hall.

Tibby didn't usually open the bakery on Sundays. In fact, ever since he became a believer many years before, he had observed the Lord's Day by doing nothing except attending services at Broad Street Church. But this Lord's Day was different. Before dawn, Tibby had come to the shop to bake a very special cake for the celebration.

Jim Copeland was always amazed at how quickly the ladies' auxiliary could put together a covered-dish meal. From late the night before until noon on that day, the ladies had put together an elaborate spread of just the right balance of meat, vegetables, breads, and desserts. Jim's mouth had been watering even before he had said the last amen.

As he led the crowd to the basement, Jim heard the voice again, *"There are many who are lost."* Instinctively, Jim looked around to find the source of the whisper, knowing full well who had spoken.

The kitchen basement looked totally different in the daylight. The hiding places that had once loomed large to Ian had refocused themselves into the background. The tables, the chairs, the refrigerator, the sink, and the pantry were now open to him, and he thought that they even invited him. The spread of food on tables down the middle of the dining hall was also well-known to him. He had tasted those very casseroles and fruit salads. In fact, he had survived on them. Suddenly he felt bad inside about something. He had indeed stolen food from this kitchen, and though he knew that the church would never make him pay for it, he felt somehow he needed to make restitution.

Pete returned to the church building just in time to see the news trucks driving away. There were still maybe a hundred cars parked around the church, and Pete studied each one, especially the rentals and the black cars. He saw no sign of Frank or his vehicle. Pete would have breathed a sigh of relief with that discovery; however, he did not know what Frank was thinking, what he would do, or whether he was still a threat to Ian.

Pete got out of his car and walked toward the church building. He just couldn't feel right until he knew that Ian was safe.

"Lieutenant!"

Pete looked up at who was calling him. "Lieutenant Lambert!"

Pete saw Tibby standing in front of his bakery.

"Mr. Thibodeaux," Pete called back. "Tibby," Pete corrected himself.

"You come join us dere in the fellowship meal." Tibby smiled at Pete and held out a beautifully decorated sheet cake with the words "Praise the Lord" written with red icing.

"Oh, thanks, Tibby. But no, I couldn't."

"Why not? Dere's more dan enough food."

"Well, I would like to speak a word of congratulations to Missus Anderson, the pastor, and Ian."

"Come." Tibby led the policeman through the alley. Tibby used his key to open the basement door.

The crowd was milling around, waiting for the ladies to finish the table preparations.

"Pete," Jim Copeland greeted him warmly.

"Pastor . . . uh, Jim, I just wanted to congratulate all of you here and make sure everything was all right," Pete explained. "I don't want to crash the party, but Tibby . . ."

"Oh, no. You're welcome here. I told you that. We're just about to bless the food, and then we'd be honored if you'd stay."

Pete remembered his T-shirt and jeans. "But I'm not dressed . . ."

"Nonsense. You'll stay. I'd like to introduce you to the rest of the congregation . . . and to Ian."

Pete realized that he had never actually met the runaway boy, but the way several of the ladies were fawning over a blond-haired child, Pete figured that it must be Ian.

Jim held up his hands to the crowd, and within a few seconds the chatter died down. "Folks, before we go to the Lord in prayer, I'd like you all to meet Lieutenant Peter Lambert of the Mobile police force." The people applauded, surprising and embarrassing Pete. "The lieutenant helped us . . . in Ian's return," Jim continued, being careful how he phrased his introduction, "and I've asked him to join our celebration today." The congregation applauded again, and Pete blushed. He didn't know what to say.

"Thank you," he finally replied.

Ian slipped away from the ladies' grasp and approached the lieutenant.

"I'm Ian." He looked up at the officer and extended his small right hand.

The innocent face warmed Pete, and he returned the handshake. Pete tousled the boy's hair and smiled. Then Ian escorted Pete to the front of the serving line.

"Let's pray." Jim bowed his head, and so did the rest of the crowd. Pete bowed his head but didn't close his eyes. "Oh, Father, we can't thank You enough for all that's happened," Jim's prayer began. "You have done a mighty miracle in our congregation, working all things out for a purpose. Thank You for bringing Ian to us, and for Hunter as well." Hunter? Pete looked around. He was a little confused, but he noticed that not a single person was surprised. He wondered if there was more to Ian's story than he knew.

"Father, bless this food. Bless this fellowship. Bless our lives and guide us. Speak to us, God." Jim paused and caught a shaky breath. "Speak again, oh, God, about what You want us to do here at Broad Street." The pastor began to sing, and as he did, the others joined with him. "Praise God from whom all blessings flow/Praise Him all creatures here below/Praise Him above ye heavenly hosts/Praise Father, Son, and Holy Ghost. " The amen was rounded out with harmonies on several octaves. It resonated in the dining hall, and Pete was impressed with its beauty; it was like nothing he had ever heard.

Pete looked up and saw Hank, the policeman from Crestview, standing near the door. As a law enforcement official himself, Pete knew that Hank was filling the role of protector and that he was probably keeping his eye on the door, making sure that the press, and perhaps others, were being carefully screened or kept out altogether. Pete looked over the heads of the crowd and nodded to Hank. Hank returned the nod. They both knew that there was a need for some scouting. Both realized that there might still be the presence of danger.

The food looked so good. Pete tried not to take too much, being the outsider, but he couldn't resist the fried chicken, the butter beans, and the homemade rolls. And of course, he would have to try the chess pie he had spotted down on the dessert table. Ian and his aunt Jo sat directly across from Pete, and he was surprised to see their bond. Jo started to cut up the slice of roast beef on Ian's plate, and Ian whispered in her ear. Apparently Jo wasn't aware that ten-year-old boys could cut up their own roast beef, but she promptly relinquished the task. Finally, Jim came and sat next to Pete.

"We are so glad you came," Jim said as he unwrapped a plastic fork and spoon from a napkin.

"Well, uh . . . I appreciate the invitation. I was really just checking, you know, on Ian."

Jim looked at Pete. "We'll talk a little later about it." Jim gave a knowing nod to Pete and then looked at Ian, who was busily eating his food.

"So, Miz Anderson, you planning on going back to Crestview today?" the pastor asked.

"Yes, Pastor. We came in Jean's car. Of course, Hank has his car here too, so we'll just caravan home." Pete and Jim were both thankful for Hank's presence there in the room and later on the road.

Ian leaned over and pulled at Jo's sleeve. He whispered something to her. Jo shook her head and then said, "Maybe later, hon."

"You looking for rest rooms, Ian?" Jim asked.

"No, sir," Ian said with a smile. "I know where they are."

Jim smiled too. "I forgot. You know this place probably better than anyone."

"Yes, sir. I was wanting to say good-bye to Mercy and Hope," Ian said after a large bite of sweet-potato casserole.

"Mercy and Hope?" Pete asked.

"Cats," Jim explained. "They're kind of . . . well, alley cats. Everybody around here feeds them. They really don't belong to anyone. I just named them Mercy and Hope." Pete understood everything except the unusual names. Most cats he had known were named Tabby or Snowflake. "I see," he finally said. Pete realized all a sudden that Hank was standing behind him.

"Lieutenant, thanks for coming," Hank began. Pete nodded a "you're welcome" response because his mouth was too full to reply. "When you're finished eating, let's talk," Hank added. Pete nodded again. He knew what the conversation would be about.

"He checked out this morning. I examined the hotel grounds. I checked out the immediate area around the church and have not seen him or his car," Pete reported.

"That's good and bad," Hank said. "I'd like to know exactly where Frank Benson is at all times."

"Me too, Officer."

Hank looked up and saw Jim Copeland coming out of the men's room. The look on the pastor's face was one of alarm. Hank watched as Jim crossed the room, scanning it thoroughly with his eyes.

"What's up, Jim?" Hank asked.

"Have you seen Ian?" Jim asked.

Both policemen shook their heads.

"Jo said he went into the bathroom to wash his hands. I turned my back for a few minutes to talk to somebody. Then I went in to check on him. He's not in there," Jim whispered but was careful not to look panicked.

The two police officers separated and flanked the perimeter of the dining hall. The pastor went back to the table where Jo was sitting. Jo was talking to some of the other ladies and did not notice him. Trying not to display his fears, Jim leaned over the table to look and see if the boy was sitting under it. Then he looked over at Hunter. That boy was still eating, sitting quietly next to his parents. Jim pretended to be helping clear plates, but he was really looking under all the tables and chairs, hoping to find a little blond head sticking out.

Hank quickly checked the sanctuary, the organ chamber, and the baptistery area. Pete stood in front of the rest room, listening for the boy's voice. Jim nonchalantly opened the pantry, hoping that Ian was playing a harmless game of hide-and-seek, but there was no boy inside the closet. Hank reentered the room and looked at Jim. The two policemen exchanged questioning looks. Hank shook his head. All three of the men wondered if this was the time to panic, but they were also somewhat ashamed that they had let this child slip away from them.

Jim looked at Jo, who was still engaged in polite conversation. He was glad she had not noticed Ian's disappearance. Jim was sure that he had locked the basement door before the worship service that morning. However, he went and tried the knob anyway. It turned, and the pastor's heart began to race. Both Pete and Hank saw Jim open the door to the alley. Pete decided to follow Jim out. Hank remained in the dining hall and scanned the crowded room again.

The two cats were devouring what looked like roast beef on a paper plate. They did not even acknowledge the men as they bounded into the alley. "Mercy and Hope, I presume?" Pete asked.

"Ian's been here," Jim said, and his chest heaved with fear.

"You go around front, and I'll check the back, Jim." Both men ran off in opposite directions.

"I can't believe this," Jim kept saying to himself. Jim wasn't sure whether to blame himself, Ian, or God. Had they been too careless? Why would God let Ian escape them? Why would Ian do this?

Pete met Jim on the other side of the building. Both shook their heads and shrugged. Ian was not on the swing set, and he was not in the cemetery.

"Ian!" Jim called, hoping that no one inside could hear his desperate call.

"Ian!" Pete joined in.

Pete looked at the weeded field, watching for movement. Jim pulled on the door handle near the playground. It was locked and bolted from the inside. Both men knew it was time to tell the crowd inside that the boy was missing. They were prepared to take blame for their carelessness, but they were hoping that it wouldn't impair the search. "This can't be happening," Pete said out loud, echoing Jim's sentiments exactly.

Entering the alley, they saw that the cats were finishing off their meaty meal. Jim opened the basement door, quickly rehearsing what he would say to the unknowing congregation. "Let me have your attention, please," he would say, trying to get the crowd quiet. "No one panic, but Ian is missing." And then he was sure that they would panic.

However, when Pete and Jim entered the dining hall, the crowd was totally silent. In fact, there was a look of amazement on the faces that they could see. Sitting where Ian had sat earlier was someone vaguely familiar to Jim. Both police officers knew his identity immediately. It was Jeremiah Mock eating from a plate that was being refilled by Ian himself.

Pete and Jim looked over at Hank, who was as mesmerized at the sight as the rest of the people in the room. Ian looked up at the pastor and Pete, who were totally puzzled as to how the man and the boy slipped in without their knowledge.

"I found him in the alley. He was hungry. I didn't think you'd mind, Pastor Jim."

Jim shook his head but was speechless, like the others. Jim was sure that this was the homeless man who had come begging at the church door two weeks before. It made sense too that this had to be the same man who had led the police to the investigation of Ian's whereabouts.

Jo was crying, but she motioned for Jim.

"Ian had been telling me that he felt bad about the food he had stolen while he was here. He was trying to figure a way to pay it back. I'd say this isn't what he was thinking when he said it, but it would probably do in God's eyes, don't you think?"

Jim felt tears on his cheeks, not just because of the moving sight of true benevolence before him, but because of the clarity of God's message. "*There are many who are lost. Do not forget them. I have not.*" Jim knew that this derelict had been forgotten by society, but that the Almighty had remembered him just the same. It was an overwhelming thought, and Jim knew he must speak to his waiting congregation.

"Folks." Jim's voice trembled. "I've got something to tell you."

"Dad, I've got something to tell you." Frank dreaded telling his father the news. Half listening to the slurred rants of his father, Frank was hoping that finally his father would talk himself into letting the issue drop. However, Frank was wrong.

"Never send a boy to do a man's job!" Charles spoke with too much clarity for Frank to ignore. "I knew you couldn't do it. That's why I had a backup plan in place."

"A backup plan?"

"Yeah, boy. Had somebody tailing you too, just in case." Charles punctuated the statement with a condescending chuckle.

Frank couldn't believe what he was hearing. A private investigator had been charting his every move and those of the other characters in this sick drama. The investigator had apparently been feeding Charles Benson with everything from license plate numbers to detailed descriptions of Ian, Jo, Jean, and Hank.

"It's over, Dad. Why can't you accept that?"

"It's never over, boy! Not till I say it's over!"

Frank was afraid to ask what that meant. But when he got the courage to ask, he was sorry that he had.

Chapter Twenty-Four

Hank Wanted to tie

a rope to Jean's car and tether it to his own. He just wanted so much to protect the newfound boy and his guardian.

"Please don't lose me in traffic. I'll be right behind you all the way, Miz Mayer," Hank warned.

Jean was glad that the sun would be behind them. As she entered the ramp to Interstate 10, she glanced in the rearview mirror and saw Hank's car close behind and, in the distance, a small crowd still waving to them outside Broad Street Church. As the church disappeared from her sight, Jean sighed.

"I feel the same," Jo said. The ladies smiled at each other. They both knew that the ordeal had been more than exhausting. It had been debilitating, invigorating, and life-changing all at the same time. The words of Jim Copeland still rang in their minds.

"We will never be the same because of this young man,"

Jim had said, rubbing the top of Ian's head. "He, without knowing it, brought us closer to the Lord and to each other. But, more than that, he brought us to a better understanding of why we're here, what our mission must be. We . . . well, I . . . have been searching for a direction in ministry. Perhaps God has a calling for us to the 'forgotten' of this world." He had looked up and finished by saying, "Thank You, Father, for reminding us."

"Aunt Jo?" Ian said softly from the backseat.

"Yes, sweet?"

"Can I open these presents now?"

Jo remembered that several people had brought gifts to Ian. Some had been wrapped and some still in store sacks, but she had placed them all in a large trash bag she had found in the church kitchen.

"Sure," Jo answered.

Ian carefully untied the bag and looked in. "Neat," he said.

"What is it?" Jean asked.

"Lots of stuff," Ian added. One by one, Ian opened the gifts. There was a children's Bible with pictures on many of the pages. There were other books, most of them with Bible stories. The books didn't look exactly new, but there was a card that read, "These were some of our children's favorite Bible storybooks. Hope you enjoy them. God Bless You, The Spiveys." Ian was truly touched by the gift. There were some packages with toys and clothes, but Ian was sure he would enjoy the Bible and the books most of all.

It all happened so fast. The big black car crossing the median didn't look out of control. It looked instead as if it were being steered in their direction. Before Jean could even react, Hank's car was speeding beside hers. Jo gasped and looked over at Hank, who was gripping his steering wheel and seemed to be bracing himself for impact. The black car slid sideways and just missed Hank, but it turned almost ninety degrees without slowing down and pulled in behind Jean's car. Hank motioned for Jean to speed up, which she did out of fear more than out of obedience. Hank jerked his wheel and wedged his car between Jean's and the black one. The black car clipped Hank's bumper, and they both skidded, fishtailing slightly but regaining control.

"What's going on?" Ian said from the backseat. Jean did not answer. Jo only said, "Oh, God, help us!"

Hank looked at the mile marker and then in his rearview mirror at the other car. Without taking his eyes off the road, he fumbled for his cell phone. He couldn't feel it on the seat next to him. He knew that he had put it there, but in the swerving it probably had fallen over between the passenger seat and the door.

The black car sped up and changed into the left lane, cutting Hank off when he tried to do the same. Hank glanced at the driver, fully expecting to see Frank Benson at the wheel. The glass was tinted enough that Hank could not see the driver clearly. At quick glance, it sort of looked like Frank, but Hank could not be sure.

The sight of the black car scared Jean so badly that she put on the brakes. Hank had anticipated that and was braking at the same time. That gave Hank time to pull into the left lane and then in between the black car and Jean. Several other approaching motorists were slowing down, and Hank prayed that someone would call the highway patrol and report them all. He was willing to, even praying to, get stopped and cited for reckless driving. He didn't know if it would affect his record or not, but he did not care. It could save the lives of the innocent, precious people he was trying to protect. Hank felt next to him on the seat again. He couldn't locate the phone. He prayed that Jo would remember her phone and perhaps call 911.

The black car sped up, and Hank was hoping that the driver was going to leave them alone. Hank wondered if he should lead Jean off at the next exit, perhaps to a police station or a hospital, someplace where officials could protect them. Just then the black car slammed on its brakes. Hank's attempt to stop was futile, and he jerked the wheel to the right, skidding his car directly into a guardrail. The impact was fierce, and Hank's last memory was of a white cloud coming toward him.

Jean instinctively jerked her wheel to the left, just missing the black car. She was too frightened to be grateful for the grassy median that her car tore into. When she applied the brakes, she felt her tires dig into soft ground.

"Everybody all right?" Jean managed to say.

"Yes." Jo turned immediately to Ian.

"Uh-huh."

"Hank? Where's Hank?" Jo suddenly remembered seeing Hank's car plow into a barrier. She opened the passenger door without thinking. Looking back, she could see Hank's car embedded in the railing. She screamed and stepped out of the car into ankle-deep mud.

"No! Jo! No!" Jean screamed.

Suddenly Jo wondered, *Where is the black car?* Looking ahead, she saw the car perhaps a hundred yards away. The front of the car was turned toward them, and it was heading directly for them.

"Get in, Jo," Jean screamed at her.

Jo quickly drew her muddy shoes back into the car and slammed the door. Jean's foot pressed on the accelerator. The tires slung mud out behind them and up onto the back window.

"We're stuck!" Jo shouted.

"Aunt Jo?" Ian finally spoke. "What are we going to do?"

Jo didn't answer. Jean gunned the motor again, only digging her tires deeper and deeper into the mud.

"Where can I go? Where can I go?" Ian began to say, almost chanting.

Jo glanced at him, and to her surprise she saw that Ian's face was not wracked with terror, but he was intently engaged in a conversation with Someone.

The black car kept moving toward them. Jean tried to accelerate once more. Her car did not budge. Jean gripped the steering wheel. Jo reached for Ian. The movement she made was just in time to avoid the crush of the passenger door. Jo's body was jolted and sent slamming into Jean's. The sudden motion kept Jo from seeing who it was that had deliberately rammed into them and was now coming at them with a gun.

Hank had no idea how he had gotten there. After a few seconds looking around him, he could tell that he was in a hospital, and from the pain that he felt practically all over his body, he knew that he had been injured somehow. He tried to remember. A bullet in a drug bust shoot-out had once grazed him, but this was different. Though they would not move, his arms and legs ached fiercely. Hank tried to raise his head to look at his own injuries, but his head began to pound, and he laid back and almost passed out. He heard a voice.

"The police officer is waking up," a female voice said from the doorway.

Hank opened his eyes and saw a familiar image come into focus.

"Hank?" Jim Copeland said. "Hank, can you hear me?"

Hank blinked, but he couldn't form words.

"Do you know what happened to you, hon?" Another voice. Another face came into focus. It was Sue Ellen. Suddenly Hank began to remember. "Where's Ian?" he tried to ask.

"Try to rest," Sue Ellen said softly.

"No, where's Ian and Jo and Jean?" Hank said, or at least he thought he said. Suddenly everybody disappeared and he fell into a painful sleep.

Frank's mind was numb as he sat in the dark cell. Finally a question came to him, *Why did I do it?* Just as he was about to sort it all out, someone spoke.

"Hey." It was Pete standing on the other side of the bars looking in. Frank looked up at his old friend.

"What's the latest?" Frank asked, afraid to hear the answer.

"Hank is critical but stable," Pete replied.

"Oh."

"Wanna talk?" Pete asked.

Frank paused and then nodded.

"Sergeant?" Pete summoned a uniformed guard, who unlocked the cell and let Pete Lambert enter.

Frank would not look at Pete when he spoke. That somehow made it easier to talk about all the horrible things that had happened.

Pete interrupted Frank's first sentence. "Before you say anything much, you need to wait for your lawyer," Pete said.

"I thought this wasn't an official interrogation. Just one friend talking to another."

"Yeah, it is, but I can't forget who I am," Pete added, referring to his position on the police force.

The sergeant appeared and announced that Frank's lawyer had arrived.

"Good," Pete said, rising from the cot next to Frank. "Frank, you need to tell your lawyer about the details. If you need me, I'll be right outside."

Burton Kelly, the Benson family's lawyer for twenty years, entered the cell with a briefcase. Laying it down on the cot, he looked at his client. "I just talked to your daddy, son. He's pretty upset with you."

Frank looked up at his lawyer, who looked him straight in the eye and asked, "Why'd you do it, boy?"

Broad Street Church was getting used to prayer vigils. This would be the third in a little over a week. The report on Hank Thomas was disturbing. His condition could go either way, they were told. The congregation prayed for his full recovery. By the time Jim got to the church, more than two hundred people had gathered and were on their knees in prayer. Abbie had come too, with Melanie's assistance, and she was sitting on the very front pew surrounded by several church members who were praying silently as Abbie prayed aloud.

"Oh, Father, You have done such marvelous things. But Lord, we just don't understand what's happening now. Please help us to put it all under Your care. You are sovereign. You are holy." It warmed Jim's heart to hear her pray. When she had finished, he touched her on the shoulder.

She looked up at him with questioning eyes.

Jim whispered to Abbie, "Hank's awake. I'm going to go back to the hospital. He needs a pastor right now." Jim noticed as he turned around to exit that everyone had stopped praying and was looking at him, waiting for some news.

"Hank Thomas is out of the coma but still in ICU. The fact that he's talking is a good sign." There were sighs of relief all over the room. "I plan to go back to the hospital now. I'll bring you word as soon as I hear," Jim said as he pushed on the door to the sanctuary. Turning around, he added, "You folks bless my heart."

Hank couldn't escape. No matter where he went, the huge white cloud followed him. He wasn't afraid, though. He knew, somehow, that the cloud had come in peace. It would not harm him. In fact, it was there to protect him. However, it kept him from seeing clearly. Beyond the cloud, Hank could faintly make out the image of Ian Lane, who was turning to run away. Hank believed that if he could only get beyond the cloud, he could keep Ian from leaving.

Suddenly a nurse was standing beside his bed. Hank knew that what he had just seen was a dream, but that fact made it no less disturbing. He had no idea how long he had slept.

Hank tried to open his mouth.

"You've got a breathing tube in, Mr. Thomas. Don't try to talk right now. The doctor is on the hall and may decide to take it out since you're awake," the nurse said confidently.

Hank tried to gesture. He was so confused. What was a dream? What was reality? What had happened? Where was Ian?

A man wearing surgeon's scrubs entered the room.

"Mr. Thomas, I'm Dr. Bragg, one of the physicians who worked on you when you first came in," the doctor said as he looked at a chart. "Do you remember what happened?"

Hank tried to speak. He remembered he couldn't, so he shook his head.

"I think we can take the breathing tube out now," the doctor said, paging a nurse who had just stepped out of the room.

Hank was so glad to have the tube out, but his throat was so raw he almost couldn't make a sound. Whispering, he asked, "What happened?"

"You were in an automobile accident on I-10. Do you remember that?"

Hank suddenly remembered.

"Seat belt and air bag helped save your life, I believe. You have a lot of broken bones and some internal injuries. You also got a broken nose from the bag's impact; however, it's better than the alternative." The doctor went about checking Hank all over. Every place the doctor touched hurt so badly that it brought tears to Hank's eyes.

"Where's Ian, Jo, and Jean?" Hank had to ask.

"Who?" the doctor asked.

"The people in the car ahead of me. What happened to them?"

"Oh, well, I'll let the people outside tell you about that." The doctor wrote something down on his chart and made a swift exit.

Hank began to remember everything—the interstate chase, his own crash—but he didn't remember anything after that. Had the man in the black car harmed his friends? Had it indeed been Frank Benson—or someone else? When the door opened again, the whole nightmare began to unfold.

"Guard!" Burton Kelly yelled. Immediately the sergeant appeared to unlock the cell door.

Pete met the lawyer in an interrogation room. "What's he saying?" Pete asked.

"He'll give a deposition," the lawyer answered. "Tomorrow. D.A. says he'll probably just be charged with conspiracy. Charles? Well, that's another thing." Burton sighed.

Pete decided it was not a good idea to go back into the cell with his friend.

"Hank," Jim said, and Hank opened his eyes. Hank managed a smile. "Thought you might like to know that there are more than two hundred people praying for you right now at the church."

Hank mouthed a feeble "thank you."

"Thank you."

Frank started when he heard the words. He knew the voice, but he was too ashamed to look up.

"Mr. Benson, you saved our lives," Josephine Anderson said quietly.

By the time Jim left the hospital, it was almost midnight. He figured that Abbie was at home and that the vigil had dispersed after he called with an update. He had encouraged his people, however, to keep praying. Hank was still very critical, and then there was the Frank Benson case.

The story was on the front page of the morning paper. Running a picture they had taken the day before, Ian's face looked out at the world. The story lead read: "Just yesterday Ian Lane was a runaway boy who had been found and returned to his guardian. Today, the boy is at the center of a series of crimes that date back ten years."

The article told about the house fire, Ed and Mary Lane's deaths, Ian running away from his guardian, and his miraculously being found in Mobile. Without speculation, the newspaper reported what had been communicated at a press conference the night before.

"I am Lieutenant Pete Lambert of Mobile City Police force. I have become a personal friend of Ian Lane, his great-aunt Josephine Anderson, her friend Jean Mayer, and their friend Hank Thomas, a police officer from Crestview, Florida. I have been asked to make a statement on behalf of the families involved." Pete swallowed hard, looked up to flashing cameras, and then continued to read from his written manuscript.

"Ian Lane was found Saturday night seeking refuge in Broad Street Church in this city. He was reunited with his guardian at that time. They left this city at approximately 4 P.M. Sunday traveling east on Interstate 10. The boy was traveling in Mrs. Mayer's car along with Mrs. Anderson. Following them in his own car was Hank Thomas. At around mile marker 48, just before they would have crossed the Florida state line, Mrs. Mayer's vehicle encountered another vehicle that had been traveling west. The other vehicle

crossed the median and reportedly was trying to force Mrs.
Mayer's vehicle off the road. Officer Thomas tried to protect Mrs. Mayer's car by placing his vehicle in between the
other two, trying to make his vehicle a barrier. After approximately one mile, Officer Thomas's vehicle was forced off
the road and into a bridge railing. Officer Thomas is in an
undisclosed hospital in critical condition. Mrs. Mayer's vehicle was forced off the interstate and landed in the
median."

"When did you come upon the accident, Lieutenant?" a
reporter interrupted. Pete looked annoyed.

"If you'll let me finish," Pete answered tersely.

"At what time did you encounter it?" another reporter
piped in.

"I'm getting to that," Pete said. "May I continue with
my full statement?" Pete didn't wait for a response.

"At around 4:45 P.M. that same day, Sunday, I had received a call from an old acquaintance of mine, Frank
Benson from Madison, Florida. He informed me of a plan
that he believed his father, Mr. Charles Benson, also from
Madison, had revealed to him that included the abduction of
and/or the murder of Ian Lane." There were flashes from
cameras and a roar of conversation. Pete looked up. The reporters quieted and he continued. "I dispatched the Alabama
Highway Patrol and asked them to look for vehicles that
met Mrs. Mayer's and Officer Thomas's description. I also
asked them to look for, and apprehend if necessary, the
black Mercedes driven by Charles Benson. However, before
AHP could apprehend, the crash of the vehicles had occurred. I arrived at the scene in my cruiser to find Mr.
Charles Benson approaching Mrs. Mayer's vehicle with a
gun." More flashes and Pete looked up at the cameras. "I
drew my revolver and commanded Mr. Benson to drop his

weapon. He complied, and law enforcement officials who had just arrived on the scene took him into custody. Charles Benson was charged with attempted murder and is now being held without bond in the Mobile County Jail. Other charges are pending. Frank Benson is also being held on conspiracy charges."

"What about the boy, Lieutenant, and the other two ladies?" a reporter pressed.

Pete gave a faint smile. "Thank God, they are safe." Pete almost broke down and cried, but he caught himself. "A full FBI investigation is being launched to examine other details related to this case. That is something that I cannot disclose at this time."

As Pete walked away from the news lectern, the questions continued:

"Is Charles Benson responsible for Ed and Mary Lane's death? Did Frank Benson conspire with his father? Why did Frank Benson call you?"

Some of these questions would be answered in the months to come. Some questions would remain forever.

Epilogue

Twenty years later

Asylum. Refuge. Sanctuary.

Haven. The congregation considered all these descriptions for their new facility. However, the name for the shelter that would minister to runaway children was never questioned. The place built on the vacant lot next to Broad Street Church would be called: "The Lane House."

The church building itself had taken new life. The sanctuary had been renovated and enlarged twice to accommodate its growing membership.

Tibby had donated his bakery to the church, and the kitchen had been converted into a hall that was feeding and ministering to hundreds of homeless people weekly. In fact, the program, "The Jeremiah Project," was being used as a model for other inner-city ministries across the country.

Outside the walls of the church, a prison ministry had developed. It not only cared for inmates at the local jails, but it had expanded as far as Fountain Correctional Center in Atmore.

After Peter Lambert's conversion, he and many other Christian law enforcement officials at the Mobile police force lived out their faith in ministries to children whose parents were serving time.

At the dedication service for the Lane House, the young pastor of Broad Street Church stepped into the pulpit. Looking at the congregation, he began, "My aunt Jo once told me, 'God is sometimes slow, but He's never late.'" Pastor Ian looked at his spiritual father sitting on the front pew and smiled. "Senior Pastor Copeland heard God speak to him twenty years ago about seeking the lost. Though God has worked mightily at Broad Street, it's taken two decades for that whispered message to become a lighthouse to the world." Abbie and the three Copeland children beamed with joy as they watched Brother Jim cut the ribbon that would officially open the doors to a haven, an asylum for children who have no other place to go.

Since 1894, Moody Publishers has been dedicated to equip and motivate people to advance the cause of Christ by publishing evangelical Christian literature and other media for all ages, around the world. Because we are a ministry of the Moody Bible Institute of Chicago, a portion of the proceeds from the sale of this book go to train the next generation of Christian leaders.

If we may serve you in any way in your spiritual journey toward understanding Christ and the Christian life, please contact us at www.moodypublishers.com.

"All Scripture is God-breathed and is useful for teaching, rebuking, correcting and training in righteousness, so that the man of God may be thoroughly equipped for every good work."
—2 TIMOTHY 3:16, 17

MOODY
PUBLISHERS

THE NAME YOU CAN TRUST®

ASYLUM TEAM

ACQUIRING EDITOR:
Michele Straubel

COPY EDITOR:
Cheryl Dunlop

BACK COVER COPY:
Julie-Allyson Ieron, Joy Media

COVER DESIGN:
UDG DesignWorks

INTERIOR DESIGN:
Ragont Design

The typeface for the text of this book is
AGaramond